For Susan, who has always had my back.

HAPPY GO LUCKY ME

A LIFETIME OF MUSIC

PAUL EVANS

An Autobiography

McNIDDER & GRACE

Published by McNidder & Grace
21 Bridge Street
Carmarthen SA31 3JS
Wales, United Kingdom

www.mcnidderandgrace.com

Original paperback first published 2021

A catalogue record for this work is available from the British Library.

ISBN 9780857162182 paperback
ISBN 9780857162199 ebook

Cover design by Tabitha Palmer
Designed by JS Typesetting Ltd
Printed and bound in the United Kingdom by Short Run Press, Exeter

Praise for *Happy Go Lucky Me*

'I always thought that Paul Evans was one of the most versatile pop songwriters – 'When' (Kalin Twins), 'Johnny Will' (Pat Boone), 'Happy Go Lucky Me' (George Formby, no less!), 'I Gotta Know' (Elvis Presley), 'Let's Pretend' (Lulu) and 'Hello This is Joannie' (Paul Evans himself). This is partly because he worked with so many co-writers. This book is a glorious love letter to those wonderful songwriters around the Brill Building in New York. Brill!'
Spencer Leigh, author and broadcaster

'The affable hit recording artist and songwriter takes us on a delightful romp through New York's magnetic music scene, with its outsized characters and personalities, from the 1950s onward. In a review of his first record, for mighty RCA Victor, *Cash Box* magazine noted that 'Paul Evans is here to stay'. What a crystal ball that reviewer had in 1957. Now he's been around long enough to tell the tales with authority and good humour.'
John Broven, author of *Record Makers and Breakers* and other award-winning books

'To be successful and survive the music Industry are two different things. In *Happy Go Lucky Me* Paul Evans writes about how he accomplished both in a riveting true story. Paul's unique first-person account tells of the trails and triumphs of a challenging and ever-changing music industry. With a passion for songwriting and publishing, Paul explores the very foundation on how his world of songwriting, radio jingles and recording was formed with a well-researched look at his predecessors during the Tin Pan Alley era and the dawn of the Brill Building. Entertaining from start to finish, Paul's book is a real page-turner, highly recommended for true music connoisseurs.'
Johnny Vallis, musician

'Paul Evans had a dream – to make his mark as a creative musical force. Here's how he made that dream come true as a singer, songwriter, producer and the crafter of three decades of hits for himself and others amid the heroes and villains and the music biz.'
Gary Theroux, author *The History of Rock 'n' Roll*

'Perhaps the name Paul Evans wouldn't be the first to trip off the tongue if you were asked to name some 50's pop singers, but here is a man who remarkably has survived in a highly competitive business from his teens to his eighties. If you want to read the most in-depth book

about the music industry and its characters from A to Z then this is the book for you.'
Roger Easterby, record producer

'This is not just a book about Paul Evans. It is so much more. I was very aware of his chart successes as a recording artiste but I never really knew him as a terrific composer who provided hits for the likes of Elvis Presley, Bobby Vinton, The Kalin Twins and more. The book takes us on a fascinating ride through the thrills, spills and vagaries of the American music industry, from the beginnings of rock and roll in the fifties and the tsunami of hits that poured out of the legendary Brill Building right up to present times. Paul thankfully doesn`t forget to include the tales of shady deals by shady people who knew exactly how to rip off young and innocent kids who were trying to make it in the business. Join the ride. Once you`re on you won`t want to get off.'
Frank Allen, bass/vocals with The Searchers and author of *Travelling Man* and *The Searchers and Me*

'I've read dozens of music business autobiographies through the years, but only a very few manage to capture the behind-the-scenes stories and larger than life characters in a way that makes us feel like we're right there in the middle of it. Paul Evans' *Happy Go Lucky Me* takes us on a magical journey which sees him writing songs with the greats of the Brill Building era, landing singles with Elvis Presley, Bobby Vinton and Lulu and topping the charts (here and around the world) as a recording artist in his own right. With candor and wit, Paul takes us from his humble beginnings and boom years through multiple reinventions in jazz, jingles and television over the course of a six-decade career that's still going strong. If you love a (true) story where indefatigable creative spirit and relentless optimism triumphs over a tough, competitive business, this one is a must read!'
Mark Fried, founder and CEO, Mojo Music & Media

'Paul Evans has done it all successfully, from Jazz to Top 40 to having a #1 Country hit on New York's WHN radio.'
Ed Salamon, former President /Programming, Westwood One Radio Networks

'I have long admired the original and very varied songs of Paul Evans and I'm looking forward to learning more about them – and him – in his memoir.'
Sir Tim Rice, lyricist and author

ABOUT THE AUTHOR

Paul Evans has had a long and varied musical career.

As a songwriter, Paul has written hits for himself as well as for Bobby Vinton ('Roses Are Red, My Love'), the Kalin Twins ('When'), and Elvis Presley (including 'I Gotta Know' and 'The Next Step Is Love').

His songs have been featured in films (Martin Scorsese's *Goodfellas* and John Waters' *Pecker*), television shows (*Scrubs*, the Hulu series *11.22.63)* and TV ads (the 1965 Clio-winning Kent commercial "Happiness Is", and campaigns for the UK's Sainsbury's and France's Intermarché supermarkets). He also wrote an off-off Broadway show, *Cloverleaf Crisis*, and the theme for the original network television show *CBS This Morning*.

Paul has spent a great deal of his life as a recording artist, first charting in 1959 with 'Seven Little Girls Sitting In The Back Seat', following up quickly with 'Midnight Special' and 'Happy Go Lucky Me', and then having a hit in 1979 with 'Hello, This Is Joannie' (#6 on the UK's pop charts, Top 40 on *Billboard*'s Country charts).

Paul has produced music tracks for recordings, industrials, jingles and television. He has also soloed and sung in groups on many commercial jingles, and has been seen and heard on the *Late Show with David Letterman* and *Late Night with Conan O'Brien*. His voice can be heard in the Woody Allen films *Mighty Aphrodite* and *Everyone Says I Love You.* He was also a part of the world-traveling jazz quintet Group 5ive.

FOREWORDS
by Frank Allen and Mark Fried

Paul Evans shot onto the charts in 1959 with 'Seven Little Girls (Sitting In The Back Seat)', a catchy earworm of a song that turned him almost overnight into a teenage idol at a time when good looking young guys were being transformed daily into eye candy for young girls to scream at and to spend their record buying money on.

But Paul was smart enough to realise that the songwriter was the one who would still be earning his rewards long after the singer`s star had faded.

He fine-tuned his craft at the iconic Brill Building in New York where hits were being churned out daily by the likes of Pomus & Shuman and Lieber & Stoller, and nearby at 1650 Broadway by Aldon writers Mann & Weill and Goffin & King.

He was to provide hits for the likes of Elvis Presley. 'I Gotta Know' was one of my favourite tracks from the *Elvis Is Back* album. 'Roses Are Red My Love' was possibly Bobby Vinton`s most remembered success. And somewhat bizarrely his own hit, the self penned 'Happy Go Lucky Me', was covered here in the UK by George Formby, a geeky ukulele playing vaudeville star of the 40s whose career was in its fading years. Nevertheless, the clever Paul was receiving the writer`s royalties from the Formby sales.

The world of show business can often be a place where shady deals are made by shady men. Tricksters whose ethos was 'a day without cheating an artiste is a day wasted'. Paul tells it like it is. Once bitten he always tried to learn from the experience to make sure he never got caught again.

People in the entertainment industry love reading fascinating stories about our own special world. I am no exception and I loved this book. I think you will too.

Frank Allen, bassist/vocals with The Searchers 1964 to the present day

The second half of the 20th century saw the American music business grow from a small group of writers, recording studios and independent labels operating within about five city blocks on New York's Broadway to a multi-billion dollar business run by huge music and media conglomerates with offices all over the world. The music itself changed, too, from ballroom standards to rock and roll, from disco to grunge, and from rap to hip-hop. And as the business evolved, songwriters and artists found themselves on the top of the heap one day only to fall to the bottom of the barrel the next as a fickle public moved on to the next big thing.

But Paul Evans is a unicorn. Starting out in the late-50s as a fledgling songwriter, competing with such Brill-era giants as Carole King, Neil Sedaka and Phil Spector, he managed to get a long list of his songs cut across multiple genres and continents by such stars as Bobby Vinton, Jackie Wilson, Roy Clark, Lulu and Elvis. And while many of the songwriters of the day tried and failed to become artists themselves, Paul made the transition seamlessly, racking up Top 10 records on both sides of the Atlantic through the 60s and 70s. As styles and sounds shifted away from traditional pop in the 80s and beyond, Paul reinvented himself as a successful jingle writer and television composer while keeping a foothold in the live circuit, touring with a vocal jazz group and delighting fans on the oldies circuit.

But *Happy Go Lucky Me* is not just a story about one man's extraordinary longevity in a decidedly mercurial business. Paul gives us a front row seat to his personal adventure, filled with larger-than-life characters, where random introductions lead to big wins or crushing failures and a quick wit and relentless optimism (not to mention a ton of talent) are the primary tools for survival. And while the backdrop is music, the artisans who produce it and the heroes and villains who determine their fate, there's a subtext here about one man's continual creative reinvention, which can apply to almost anyone in any professional field. So sit back and let Paul take you through his six-decade adventure in one of the most dynamic, unpredictable, cutthroat but ultimately rewarding professions in the world. I guarantee you'll enjoy the ride.

Mark Fried, founder and CEO, Mojo Music & Media

CONTENTS

INTRODUCTION

MUSIC, MUSIC, MUSIC

I was born Paul Lyle Rapport on March 5, 1938 into an unusually musical family. Let's take my mother, Leah, for instance. She played piano in a band that worked the Catskill Mountains resort area in upstate New York. Later she taught piano and played in silent movie theaters. She told me how her father would accompany her to the theaters because at that time theaters had movable chairs, and somehow those chairs occupied by men kept sliding closer and closer to the pretty piano player. It was my mother who made sure that my sisters and I all took piano lessons. So, okay, I was off to a good musical start.

The other half of my musical genes comes from my father, Nathan. He was a creative artist and lettered the famous poster for *Gone With The Wind* while he was working for MGM Studios. He wrote poetry and drew cartoons for *The Flutist* magazine. He played the flute as a hobby, and here's a bit of family history: my father sold his flute to pay for my first guitar. He sold it at such a fair price that the buyer ran off with the flute before my father could change his mind. How could I not love that first Guild guitar?

I was the youngest of three children. My eldest sister, Estelle, taught me the basics of chording a guitar. She was a folkie, and in demand at hootenannies. Even though she was twelve years older than I was, she would even allow me occasionally to accompany her to these folk song sing-alongs. That's how I acquired my early love of folk music. Years later I gave my Guild guitar to Estelle. The family would gather at her home and we'd have our own hootenannies. And when Estelle passed away, my niece inherited the guitar, so now

My first Guild Guitar

we gather at her home for a family sing-along whenever we can. The tradition continues, and the guitar has become a family heirloom.

Our family's middle sibling, Marilyn, made a career playing the piano for private parties and in clubs and stores. She played for years at Nordstrom, the large luxury department store chain. Marilyn had an incredible "ear" for music. She could play any standard song you could name, and maybe even more impressively, play it in the key that you might want to sing it in. Just ask her, and voilà, Marilyn would play it for you.

I once wrote a song with my father after he passed away. Impossible? Not at all! Allow me to explain. Dad had written a little ditty that my sisters and I loved. I found it in a stack of memorabilia after he died and added a couple of verses to it. It told our family's story:

'I LOOK AT THE MOON'

I look at the moon, the moon looks at me
And then we two we look at the sea
The sea sees we, we see the sea
Dum diddle diddle dum dum dee

Now this little ditty was written by my daddy
As he dawdled one day on a doodlin' pad
He probably wrote it to cheer us all up
When me and my sisters were feelin' real bad
Now Estelle is the oldest, I am the youngest
Marilyn's in the middle—and still when we're sad—
There's a trick that we've found that can turn it around
We just sing a little bitty of this ditty by Dad

* * *

Dad was a flautist, and Mom was the proudest
Of her children, including her loudest—who could that be?
Estelle plays guitars, Marilyn plays the bars
And I play for people who like oldies like me
Our family tradition, our musical mission
Is to play and to sing at the drop of a hat
And Mother and Father, did we ever bother
To sit you both down and to thank you for that?

I look at the moon, the moon looks at me
And then we two we look at the sea
The sea sees we, we see the sea
Dum dum diddle diddle dum dum dee

Nathan Rapport and Paul Evans.
Published by Port Music, Inc.

Dinnertime was family time with my mother and father, my sisters and my grandmother. My favorite seasons were spring, summer, and fall because we would eat in our screened-in porch overlooking our vegetable garden and lilac trees while we listened to the sounds of Perry Como, Dinah Shore, Doris Day, and other popular singers of the day on our radio. However, those peaceful meals came to a screeching halt when I discovered rock 'n' roll.

My father was a Gilbert and Sullivan fan. When their music was played on WQXR, New York's classical music station, he would sing along, word for word. He could tolerate the folk music that my sister Estelle brought into the house, but when I asked if we could listen to the beginnings of rock 'n' roll—Elvis, Little Richard, Chuck Berry, Bo Diddley, etc.—my father tried but couldn't abide the music. So he bought me my own radio and banished it and me

Performing at my high school's Valencia Theater show

to our basement. I can still remember him standing at the top of the stairs and yelling, "Turn that damn radio down."

I went into the basement willingly, and started my exile by tuning in to *Barkin' With Larkin*, Don Larkin's country music show on WAAT, a New Jersey station that reached across the Hudson River into New York City. That's where I heard an early interview with Elvis Presley. However, as rock 'n' roll took the place of the standard songs on local radio, I quickly became devoted to WINS with Alan Freed and Murray Kaufman, WMGM with Peter Tripp, and eventually WABC's Dan Ingram and WMCA's "Good Guys" who dominated the '60s. All of them were my NYC rock 'n' roll heroes.

The basement became some sort of an office for me. I added a phonograph player and a tape recorder, and that hideaway became a hangout for my friends who were into music. The tape recorder, by the way, replaced a wire recorder that my father had given me and which I used to record my first writing attempts. I'd record my songs onto a moving spool of wire. Really. *Onto a spool of wire.* The trouble with the wire recorder (besides its sound quality) was that if you were in "fast forward" or "reverse" and hit "stop", the wire would often wrap itself around its spool and you'd wind up with one big unusable tangle of wire. Thank goodness (sometimes) that tech marches on.

I went to P.S. 136 in my hometown of St. Albans in Queens, New York, and then to Andrew Jackson High School in bordering Cambria Heights, where I wound up producing and singing in our school's variety shows. Yes, I was some sort of a "Mr. Entertainment" at Jackson, but I plead guilty to being jealous of our school's other male singer. He was a tall, good-looking guy who crooned love songs and was rewarded with screams from the girls in the audience. My appearances were applauded—but where were the screams? Later, just a year after graduation, I caught sight of the crooner in an advertisement for Thomas' *Hairpieces*. Poof! The teenage envy that I had been carrying around with me was gone.

Our variety show's biggest moment came in 1955, when we held it at the Valencia Theater in the nearby town of Jamaica, where my family would go for our major shopping. The Valencia was the first of five Loew's "Wonder Theaters"; very large and lavishly decorated theaters located in and around New York City, built in

1929 and 1930. It was the largest of the Wonder Theaters, meant to hold 3,500 people, and was called by some "the Taj Mahal of movie theaters". Stepping out on that stage was an awesome moment for me and, I'm sure, for my fellow performers. The show was hosted by New York City's popular WMGM disc jockey Bill Silbert, and I continued my role of producer, MC and singer. I was now one very small step closer to a career in music.

And here's a bit of trivia for you. The Shangri-las, who recorded 'Leader of the Pack' and 'Remember (Walking in the Sand)' got their career started when they were attending Andrew Jackson High School in 1963.
Go Andrew Jackson!!
(And go Andrew Jackson did—when the city closed it in 1994.)

I graduated from high school and went on to Columbia University on a partial scholarship to study engineering. While there I hosted a weekly folk music show on Columbia's own AM radio station, WKCR-AM. (This was a "carrier current" system, which was broadcast through the university's electrical system and could only be heard on AM radios that were plugged into outlets on campus. My audience was obviously limited.) The big folk-pop music revolution hadn't gotten under way yet, so I played mostly Pete Seeger and the Weavers, Harry Belafonte and Burl Ives. I taped my first show and when I listened back I realized that not only was my voice New York-heavy, I delivered my comments with such New York speed that I had trouble understanding myself. I spent the rest of the semester practicing how not to speak like a New Yawker. Unfortunately, my out-of-town friends tell me that I still haven't solved the problem.

After that first year at Columbia, I got my first taste of singing professionally. My friends and I used to swim at the Rockaway beaches in Queens. We'd take the same streets to get there and back, and we would drive passed Basile's, a small nightclub owned by the Basile brothers, Ed and Jack. One day, curiosity and thirst got the better of us and we stopped in for a beer. We noticed that the club had a bar and a dining room with a small stage open to the two rooms. After a couple of visits, we got to know the owners while

Performing at Basile's

they tended to the bar. It turned out that they didn't get much use out of the stage, so along with my best friends, Kenny Riches and Billy Stio, I hatched a scheme to get me an audition at the club. We sat at the bar with a couple of beers and Kenny and Billy started chatting up the Basile brothers and Vera, the barmaid. They told the brothers what a good a singer I was, with me mumbling something like "Aw shucks" every once in a while. Then they "convinced" me to go back to the car and get my guitar and sing some songs for the brothers, who liked what they heard and hired me. I now had my first *paying* entertaining gig. Singing in front of a paying audience was a revelation to me: The applause was intoxicating, and I was thrilled when so many customers told me that they came to Basile's specifically to hear me. The die had been cast.

I spent my summer entertaining there. I had no car at the time, so Kenny offered to do the driving. He would pick me up at my home, drive me to Basile's, go back home to study for summer classes at City College, then come back and pick me up at 1:00 a.m. and drive me back to my home. Sometimes we'd stop along the way to debate politics or religion. Kenny continued this routine until one of the Basile brothers sold me my first car for $50.00. (Kenny and I are still buddies all these years later. My wish for the people that I care for is that they all find a Kenny in their lives.)

Some time that summer of 1956, I heard Roy Orbison's big hit recording of 'Ooby Dooby' and I loved it. The chorus went like this:

> Ooby dooby, Ooby dooby, Ooby dooby, Ooby dooby
> Ooby dooby dooby dooby dooby, Dooby do-wah,
> do-wah-do-wah

Written by: Dick Penner and Wade Lee Moore.
Published by Hi Lo Music Inc.

And I thought, *I can do that*. Perhaps not as well as the great Roy Orbison, but *I can do that.* (No one really knew just how great a singer Roy was until we heard 'Pretty Woman', 'Crying', 'Only the Lonely', 'It's Over', 'Blue Bayou' and so many other great songs that he co-wrote with either of his two favorite co writers, Bill Dees and Joe Melson.) So, I decided to do what I knew had to be done. I would take a year off from studying at Columbia and go into Manhattan to a place that I'd heard about. A building that somehow was calling to me: the Brill Building.

First I had to tell my family that I'd be giving up what was by now a full scholarship to Columbia. It was not an easy thing to do. A family meeting was called and the verdict was: "Don't." My father was furious. My brother-in-law called me stupid. I heard "What about your scholarship?" and "You're throwing away a steady career for a roll of the dice." My mother was dumbfounded. Her son wanted to be a *singer*? A *writer*? Those were supposed to be hobbies.

I left the meeting downhearted, so I arranged a meeting with my close pals, Kenny and Billy. We drove around for a while and then I parked the car and presented them with my dilemma. I had heard my family's arguments and wondered if they were correct. *Was I being stupid?* My friends were quick to warn me that if I didn't follow my dream, I'd always wonder what might have been and I would never forgive myself for not trying. Ah, thank you, thank you, my two good friends.

There were two more voices that I needed to hear. First I went to the Dean of Engineering at Columbia. "Why did you choose engineering?" he asked. I admitted that it was because I hadn't set my mind on any specific profession and had heard that engineers made a lot of money. His answer surprised me. "Paul, engineers start out at a higher income, but within four years the average business graduate makes much more money." *Oh, m'God. Another good reason for me to take a year off from school.* Then I went back to Andrew Jackson and looked up a man I trusted and had a great deal of respect for—my grade counsellor. I told him that I planned to take off just one year and if I didn't have success as a writer or singer in that first year, I'd return to college. Dependable Mr. Blatt gave me his blessings but made me promise to follow my one-year rule and, if things didn't work out, go back to my studies. That did it. My path was decided. So with apologies to my family and thanks to my friends and advisors, all that was left for me to do was to find the right spot to start my journey to music's proverbial fortune and fame.

Chapter 1
A BRIEF HISTORY OF TIN PAN ALLEY AND THE BRILL BUILDING

TIN PAN ALLEY

The name "Tin Pan Alley" originally referred to a block of five buildings on West 28 Street, between Fifth and Sixth Avenues in New York City, where writers and publishers gathered in the very early 1900s. Those buildings apparently got their name because of the cacophony created by so many pianos playing so many different melodies at the same time. I've read stories, all unverifiable, that the great songwriter Harry Von Tilzer rigged his piano by placing something—paper? tacks on a strip of cloth?—on the strings of his piano to create a more percussive sound, which certainly would have added to the noise. One reporter said that the buildings sounded like tin pans being beaten with a stick, and the name "Tin Pan Alley" was born.

Tin Pan Alley marked the centralization of the music publishing industry. Until publishers gathered together in New York City, they could be found in every major city throughout the country. Piano sales had soared following the Civil War and publishing was totally a business of selling sheet music. Local sales were limited to schools, churches and home studies. That's why local publishers were often a part of a printing business or perhaps a music store. If a song became a local hit, it was frequently bought up by a large New York City publishing firm such as Harms, Inc. or M. Whitmark & Sons, both located in Tin Pan Alley.

At this time, the late nineteenth and early twentieth centuries, over 2.5 million Eastern-European Jewish immigrants entered America, driven from their homelands by persecution and a lack of economic opportunity. Many gathered together in New York City, where they were free to maintain their cultural heritage and traditions. And music had always been a part of those traditions, from the religious (cantorial singing) to the profane (the Yiddish Theater). It is easy to see why so many Jews wound up in the music writing and publishing business.

A good example is the great Jewish-American songwriter Irving Berlin.

He was born Israel Beilin on May 11, 1888 in Russia. One of eight children, he came to America when his family immigrated to New York in 1893. When his father died, Berlin, who was just 13 years old, worked as a busker, singing for pennies. His first published song, 'Marie from Sunny Italy', appeared in 1907, and by 1911 he had his first major international hit, 'Alexander's Ragtime Band'. His songs defined American popular music for most of the 1900s, topped off by 'God Bless America' in 1918, his tribute to his beloved country, written in the same year that he became an American citizen.

So many Jewish publishers had gathered in the city of New York that it was easy for those Jewish immigrants with any musical creativity to find a home for their talents. This was certainly not the case for talented black writers who came up from the South looking for work. The one major exception was Scott Joplin. He was probably born in Texarkana, Texas in the late 1860s and became known as the King of Ragtime. He wrote the songs 'The Entertainer' and the biggest selling ragtime song ever, 'The Maple Leaf Rag'. Ragtime music was most popular in the late 1800s and early 1900s and paved the way for the names of black ragtime writers and performers like Eubie Blake and Jelly Roll Morton to enter into the public lexicon.

Publishers hired song pluggers to pitch their songs to live performers like vaudeville acts and Broadway shows. Eventually the invention of the phonograph and records added to the need for more music, and more and more publishers started to fill the need. While researching for this book, I was knocked out by the truly amazing number of memorable songs that came out of Tin Pan

Alley in the early 1900s. OMG, it boggles the mind. I'll name just a few, random examples here:

> 'The Sidewalks of New York' by Charles B. Lawlor and James W. Blake (1894)
> 'Hello Ma Baby (Hello Ma Ragtime Gal)' by Ida Emerson and Joseph E. Howard (1899)
> 'A Bird in a Gilded Cage' by Arthur J. Lamb and Harry Von Tilzer (1900)
> 'In the Good Old Summer Time' by Ren Shields and George Evans (1902)
> 'Bill Bailey, Won't You Please Come Home' by Huey Cannon (1902)
> 'Give My Regards to Broadway' by George M. Cohan (1904)
> 'Take Me Out to the Ball Game' by Albert Von Tilzer (Harry Von Tilzer's younger brother) and Jack Norworth (1908)
> 'Shine on, Harvest Moon' by Nora Bayes and Jack Norworth (1908)
> 'By the Light of the Silvery Moon' by Gus Edwards and Edward Madden (1909)
> 'Let Me Call You Sweetheart' by Beth Slater Whitson and Leo Friedman (1910)
> 'Down by the Old Mill Stream' by Tell Taylor (1910)
> 'Peg o' My Heart' by Fred Fisher and Alfred Bryan (1913)

In December 2019, New York's Landmarks Preservation Commission voted to landmark the five buildings on the north side of 28th Street for their importance to the birth of popular music.

THE BRILL BUILDING

New York City is a constantly changing city. Publishers and writers eventually made their way up to the West 49th Street area. The Brill Building centered this new Tin Pan Alley. It was the place where dreams could come true. So off to the Brill I went.

No doubt about it, I was scared. I dressed up in a jacket and tie for this new adventure. I tuned my guitar, took a deep breath and headed for the corner to pick up a bus that would take me to Jamaica, Queens, where I could catch the "E" subway train to "the city"—Manhattan—and to the Brill Building. (Many people in the outer boroughs of Queens, Brooklyn, the Bronx and Staten Island, all part of New York City, get upset when people who live in or visit Manhattan refer to Manhattan—and only Manhattan—as "The City.")

I got off the subway at 50th Street, walked east one block, around the corner, and there she was! What a beauty. The Art Deco style building with its ornate brass entrance and carved brass elevator doors stands on Broadway between 49th and 50th streets. It was built by real estate developer Abraham Lefcourt in 1931 and was originally named the Alan E. Lefcourt building in honor of his teenage son Alan, who had passed away shortly before construction began. A polished bronze bust of Alan sits atop the building's entrance. Lefcourt subleased the building lot from the Brill brothers, Samuel, Max and Maurice, who were successful haberdashers. When he defaulted due to the Depression in 1932, the brothers took possession of the eleven-story building, changed its name to the Brill Building and opened a men's clothing store on the ground floor. Although the building was sold in 2013 and has been renovated, the beautiful Art Deco entrance, elevator doors and bust of Lefcourt's son, Alan, have been left in place.

The building was intimidating, but when I looked at the listing of tenants, I knew that I had indeed come to the right place to begin my search for a future as a songwriter/singer. The building was bursting with publishers and writers. I chose a few publishers' names at random and knocked on their doors, ready to play them some songs and have them invite me in to appreciate my writing and singing skills. Unfortunately, that's not how it worked out. The doors were opened by old-line publishers who were only into standard popular songs that would attract the likes of Nat King Cole, Dinah Shore, Perry Como, Eddie Fisher, and Sinatra. They saw an 18-year-old kid holding a guitar case, looking for a live audition. None of them were in the mood for what was sure to be a lesson in rock 'n' roll, which must assuredly be a flash in the pan and would most certainly be out of style in a few months anyway. The doors slammed shut.

How depressing. Was my dream destined to last for just one day? But wait a minute! On the way out, I looked at the listing of building tenants and noticed the Audiosonic Recording Studio. The dream was still alive! Perhaps a disc in a kid's hand would be more professional and wouldn't scare any of the publishers as much as a kid with guitar in his hand did. I made a recording, showing off my singing talents on some popular hits of the day like Eddie Fisher's 'Cindy, Oh Cindy' and Harry Belafonte's 'Matilda', and my writing ability with a couple of my own songs. Audiosonic wasn't really set up to record final, release-worthy masters. But it was a convenient and friendly place to record demonstration records.

I was confident when I returned to the Brill the next day that this time knocking on doors would work. But once again, no one seemed interested. In fact, when one publisher answered my knock by telling me that they were too busy to listen to my demonstration recording, I peeked around him and saw a few people sitting around, playing poker. The whole building seemed filled with people just biding their time, waiting for rock 'n' roll to go away. Most of them had no idea about the rock 'n' roll hurricane that was coming their way. Just as I was about to call it a day, I knocked on the door of the Fred Fisher Music Company.

Fred Fisher had been a very successful songwriter in the early 1900s with songs like 1913's 'Peg o' My Heart', 1917's 'They Go Wild, Simply Wild, Over Me', and 1922's 'Chicago (That Toddlin' Town)'. He formed Fred Fisher Music, which was run by his sons Marvin and Danny Fisher after 1942. Marvin wrote 'When Sunny Gets Blue' (with lyrics by Jack Segal) for his friend, the popular recording artist Sunny Gale, but her manager turned it down. That was one bad decision, because the song became a major hit for Johnny Mathis in 1956. Fred also had a daughter, Doris Fisher, who wrote 'You Always Hurt the One You Love', a big hit for the Mills Brothers in 1944.

When I knocked on the Fred Fisher Company's door, the office manager, Stan Cooper, opened it and didn't slam it shut. He invited me in to play my demonstration recording for him and Danny Fisher, and they liked it. This is a bit embarrassing for me to relate, but one of my original songs that I included on the disk was called 'Swish Me, Baby'. Poor naïve me thought it was clear that the "swish" in the title referred to the sound made by the popular crinoline petticoats worn under the full skirts that girls wore as they swirled around the dance floor. Unfortunately, the title drew lots of laughs and Danny and Stan had to explain the blue connotation of 'swish' to me. (At the time, 'swish' was a derogatory term for gay males.) However, awkward start aside, it wasn't long before I was signed to a songwriting contract and a management contract, and Stan was eager to promote his new singer/writer.

But the first thing Stan did was to insist that I had to change my last name to a more professional-sounding one. I couldn't argue that the name Rapport didn't keep getting mispronounced. I remember my mother often replying when asked if her name was Rappaport, "No, it's Rappaport without the pap."

So Stan and I walked around the Brill Building looking for inspiration for my new name until we came to Redd Evans' publishing office. Redd was also a songwriter with a catalog that included 'There I've Said It Again', 'No Moon at All', 'Don't Go to Strangers' and 'American Beauty Rose'. "How does 'Evans' sound to you?" Stan asked. Well, if Stan liked it, I liked it. Bad choice! It turns out that *Paul Evans* is a very common name. In fact, I once joined a *Paul Evans* club on Facebook, made up solely of people named Paul Evans. Once, someone else named Paul Evans owed the IRS some money and I received threatening letters from that were meant for him. And another time our doorbell rang, my wife Susan opened the door, and two women strode past us and into our apartment. They said, accusingly, 'This doesn't look like what we expected the Paul Evans Furniture Design Studio to look like.' I envy my friend Johnny Tillotson his name.

I don't know why name changing became an imperative for many actors and singers when they entered the entertainment field. Perhaps it was a matter of jazzing up the individual's name or perhaps to Anglicize his or her name to appeal to a larger portion of the public. Another incentive could be that the Screen Actors Guild, which covers singers as well as actors, has always had a rule that forbids two members from having the exact same professional name. However, if you wish to join the union under your legal name, the union can't stop you. Reasons aside, I do remember thinking how cool it was when Simon & Garfunkel changed back to their birth names from Tom and Jerry ('Hey, School Girl', 1957). I was taking a new name because my birth name was often mispronounced, but even so I don't believe that my mother and father were particularly pleased when I gave them the news.

The second thing Stan did was to chop off a year from my age. His reasoning was that younger is always better in the pop music field where your audience is made up primarily of teenage girls. That might have been a realistic reason for making that one-year change, but for many years after that I honestly couldn't remember how old I was without counting up from my birthday on my fingers.

RCA, DECCA and ATCO RECORDS

After taking care of the obligatory changing of his artist's name and age, Stan got down to business. He knew two of RCA Victor's top

One of my first publicity pictures

executives, Brad McCuen and Steve Sholes, who were in charge of signing artists at RCA records. Stan took me over to meet and audition for the two men, who signed me immediately to a recording contract. Looking back, the speed with which they signed me is not too surprising. The independent labels were having success with singer/writers and the major labels wanted a piece of the action. Still, though, it was unbelievable to me. Think of it: I had been in the music business for only a short while and I had already signed three contracts: publishing, management and now recording! Things were happening faster than I could have imagined.

The next step, of course, was a recording session at the RCA studios. And what a group of musicians RCA hired to perform on my first ever session! Among them was Mickey Baker on guitar, fresh from his Mickey & Sylvia hit 'Love Is Strange', Everett Barksdale also on guitar, Sam "The Man" Taylor on tenor sax, "Panama" Francis on drums and Ernie Hayes on piano. I was definitely intimidated because these musicians on this, my first professional recording session, were so well known and respected, I was afraid they might judge me inadequate. I ended up so thankful to have had these recording session superstars there: they recognized that I was nervous about singing in their company and they chatted me up and calmed me down.

My first record was finally released: 'What Do You Know?', one of the songs that were on my original demonstration recording. It was backed with 'Dorothy', written by Lincoln Chase, who was eventually to write LaVern Baker's 'Jim Dandy' and Shirley Ellis's 'The Name Game'. The record was scheduled to be released on Groove Records, RCA's R & B label. Why was a white bread singer like me scheduled to have his songs released on an R & B label? Well, it seems that RCA had a marketing department, and they decided—sight unseen—that I was black. That's where RCA's marketing department was at the time, confused, and maybe even frightened by the new directions that rock 'n' roll was taking. It was overruled: the two ultimate decision makers at RCA, Sholes and McCuen, came to the record session, took one listen, and decided to release the record on the parent company's label, RCA Victor Records.

For various reasons the release of the record was held up for several months while I hung out at home or at the Fisher office, writing songs and biting my nails. When it was finally released, it suffered a terrible death, going *nowhere*. Still, I do have a handy excuse for its demise. RCA Victor Records was a very hot label at the time. They sent me on the road, where their local promotion man would take me around to radio stations and introduce me to the disc jockeys or program directors. Then, after handing over a copy of my record, they'd grin and say enthusiastically, "Look what else I have for you", and then pull out the latest by Elvis Presley, Harry Belafonte, Perry Como or some other multi-hitmaker. My record was D.O.A.

The company also booked my very first arena performance, if you call standing in front of a microphone and lip-synching, a performance. It was in a venue in Ohio in the bad old days when we lip-synched to 45 rpm singles. As you might guess, the record was defective and repeated one line over and over again. I didn't know how to handle the situation, so I jumped around the stage and made funny faces, all the time feeling like an idiot. The audience of a couple of thousand people laughed at my situation and my antics. Great: just out of the gate and already blown out. What a depressing plane ride home that was.

RCA released two more singles of mine. The first was my song 'Looking for a Sweetie', backed with 'Any Little Thing', written by Sid Jacobson and Jack Reardon. Jack went on to write the lyrics to a French melody by Sasha Distel, and 'The Good Life' became a big hit for Tony Bennett and a standard that was recorded by many other top recording artists. Sid co-authored Earl Grant's beautiful hit 'The End' with Jimmy Krondes, who would write 'Valerie' with me, a local New York doo-wop hit by the Mello-Kings that made it onto the lower end of the national charts.

The second, my song 'Caught', was backed with 'Poor Broken Heart', written by Clyde Otis and James Deliston. Clyde Otis was a major producer and writer. He co-wrote 'It's Just a Matter of Time' and 'Endlessly' for Brook Benton and 'Looking Back' for Nat King Cole. (I couldn't find James Deliston listed as a writer on any other songs.) My records got some play, but not enough to impress RCA, so they soon released me from my contract.

In spite of RCA not working out, Stan was still a believer, and he walked me over to Decca Records where Jack Reardon's and my song 'When', recorded by the Kalin Twins, had just crashed the

Top Ten. A first hit song for both of us, it had made us truly *Brill Building songwriters*. What a feeling! More of that first hit song later, but first a couple more disappointing experiences for me at two more record labels.

I cut two of my own songs, 'I Think About You All the Time' and 'Oh No', for Decca Records. It was their turn to be the hot record company in town and it turned out that 'I Think About You All the Time' was their sixth bestselling record. The five ahead of it were all on the national charts. Domenico Modugno's 'Volare' was five weeks at #1! Therefore, #6 was deemed a failure to Decca. I only found out about this when I performed at a concert at a college in Canada and the fans yelled for me to sing the song. Unfortunately I wasn't prepared. Decca hadn't told me about how close to becoming a hit it had come. Instead, they released me.

My next step was at Atco Records, where Jerry Wexler and Ahmet Ertegün signed me to their label. Atco was an abbreviation for their major label, Atlantic Records, and was intended for artists that didn't fit Atlantic's format of R & B, blues and jazz. Atlantic's best-known artists were Ray Charles and eventually Aretha Franklin. Atco's were the Coasters and Bobby Darin.

I had two record releases on Atco. Three of my own songs 'At My Party' backed with 'Beat Generation', and 'Long Gone' backed with 'Mickey My Love', (by Michael Coldin and Tony Prescott). But once again, the records failed and I found myself without a label. I've always been sad that I didn't have any success on Atco, because I liked and respected Jerry and Ahmet so much and because they were fun. Once when I was showing a new song of mine for them, they whooped and hollered and jumped all around their office. Jerry even got on his hands and knees under his desk, singing along with the demo. When the demo ended, they both immediately quieted down and said they really didn't like the song and would pass on it. My brain reeled for days from that experience.

DOWN—BUT NOT FOR LONG

Those record disappointments were big heartaches for me. But nothing can cure the blues like a big, fat hit song. Stan Cooper had just left Fred Fisher Music to form his own company, Sounds

Music. Jack Reardon and I used his new office in the Brill Building to write when Stan wasn't there. Among the songs that we wrote in that room was one called 'When'. We recorded it on a small portable tape machine with me playing an acoustic guitar and singing the lead, and Jack singing harmonies. That was it. We recorded the song once through with no instrumental and no frills. We played the recording for Stan, who loved it and immediately brought the tape to Jack Pleis, the Decca Records' Artist and Repertoire (A & R) man in charge of the Kalin Twins career, and here's how the song became a hit:

The Everly Brothers were the rage on Archie Bleyer's Cadence Records at that moment in time. Fame is very fickle in pop music. Today we know that the Everlys were an exception to that rule, their career lasting much longer than most pop careers. Back then, though, every record company in America was looking for the *next* Everly Brothers. Decca Records thought it had found the answer in the Kalin Twins. So in 1958, Decca brought the twins—Hal and Herb—to New York City for a meeting with their A & R man, Jack Pleis. However, Pleis was late, so he left a message for the twins to go through a pile of demonstration recordings of songs that he had accepted for them. Fortunately for Jack, me, and the Kalin Twins, the boys got into the wrong pile—the "Rejected" pile. There they found Jack's and my demo of 'When', and they loved it. When Pleis got back to the office, he found the twins singing the song. He was too embarrassed to admit that he had rejected it for them. To his credit, he wrote an outstanding arrangement featuring the sound of claves—and that is the true story of how 'When' became a big international hit. The song reached #5 on the *Billboard* Hot 100 but topped the charts in the UK and was covered by artists in every major country in Europe. It had a revival in 1977, when Showaddywaddy, an English group that specialized in covering hits of the '50s and '60s, took it to #3 on the UK charts.

Hal Kalin died in a traffic accident on August 24, 2005. A few months later, Herb and I spoke about touring together. We thought the fans would appreciate hearing the writer and the singer of 'When' performing together. But we never got the chance because Herb passed away suddenly, less than a year after his twin brother, on July 21, 2006.

THE CREAM OF THE BRILL BUILDING'S SONGWRITER CROP

Just one hit song, and I became a recognized figure walking among the group of songwriters that made their way through the hallowed halls of the Brill Building. Until then, it had been like I wasn't even there. No looks, no nods, no smiles, no nothing as I made my way in and out of the building. And of course I brown-bagged my lunch. But that day was over. Instantly—and I mean instantly, once 'When' hit the charts—publishers were inviting me to lunch with them at Dempsey's Restaurant in the Brill Building, owned by the fabled boxer Jack Dempsey.

In the Brill Building I found myself in the company of some great songwriters like Doc Pomus and Mort Shuman, who were coming off their top hits 'Turn Me Loose' by Fabian and 'A Teenager In Love' by Dion. But they were just warming up, because in their immediate future were more top-selling records, many of them rock 'n' roll standards: 'Viva Las Vegas' by Elvis Presley, 'Hushabye' by the Mystics, and 'This Magic Moment' and 'Save the Last Dance for Me' by the Drifters.

Pomus got his start singing in blues clubs. He also recorded the blues for some small labels, but he didn't have much success as a recording artist. Because he was getting older and had to use crutches (he lost the use of his legs to polio), labels lost interest. So Doc began writing R & B songs—with some pretty impressive results. He wrote for Big Joe Turner and for Ray Charles. He collaborated with Jerry Leiber and Mike Stoller on the Coasters' hit 'Young Blood'. Then, once he had taught the basics of songwriting to the teenage Mort Shuman, the team's songs took off—and the team of Pomus and Shuman made rock 'n' roll history together.

In 1968, Mort co-wrote the English lyrics for the off-Broadway musical that featured the songs of Jacques Brel, *Jacques Brel is Alive and Well and Living in Paris*. Mort also acted in the production, which ran at the Village Gate in Greenwich Village for four years. The revue also played in London's West End and spawned a film version in 1975. Jacques Brel was a Belgian-born singer/songwriter, well known in French-speaking countries; *Jacques Brel is Alive and Well* put him on the English-speaking map as well.

Also in the Brill Building were Ellie Greenwich and Jeff Barry. Each had written with other writers before they were married, but as a team they poured it on. They wrote such rock 'n' roll standards as: 'Da Doo Ron Ron' and 'Then He Kissed Me' for the Crystals; 'Baby I Love You' and 'Be My Baby' for the Ronettes; 'Chapel of Love' for the Dixie Cups (written with Phil Spector); 'Leader of the Pack' for the Shangri-Las; and 'I Can Hear Music' for the Ronettes and the Beach Boys.

And there's more. They discovered Neil Diamond and produced Neil's song, 'Cherry, Cherry' for him. They co-wrote 'River Deep – Mountain High' with Phil Spector for Ike and Tina Turner. Good Lord. I'm out of breath and can't tell you the dozens of other hit songs that they wrote for a long list of recording artists. I can assure you, though; it's a very substantial list. After they divorced, Ellie wrote the Broadway musical *Leader of the Pack*, based on her personal experiences in the music business.

On August 19, 2002, Susan and I went to hear Brian Wilson of the Beach Boys at B.B. Kings' nightclub on 42nd Street in Manhattan. We were seated at a front row "music table" with Ellie. One of the songs that Brian sang as part of his concert was 'Be My Baby', written by Ellie. She looked so proud. At another point during his show, Brian introduced Ellie to the audience to a big round of applause, praising her and the great songs that she had written. He then looked at her while he ad-libbed her song 'Chapel of Love'. Ellie was so honored that she couldn't control the tears of joy that poured from her eyes. The connection between singer and writer was awesome.

Perhaps the biggest of the Brill building songwriting teams were Jerry Leiber and Mike Stoller. Their partnership started when they were both 17 and they discovered that they shared a passion for the blues. As songwriters and record producers, Leiber and Stoller were there at the beginnings of the Brill Building's rock 'n' roll era. The list of their smash hit songs reads like the history of rock 'n' roll: 'Love Me', 'Jailhouse Rock', and 'Hound Dog' for Elvis Presley (Elvis' 'Hound Dog' was a cover of Big Mama Thornton's original version, which was a little "naughtier" than Elvis' version); 'There Goes My Baby' and 'On Broadway' for the Drifters; Ben E. King's solo hits 'Spanish Harlem' and 'Stand by Me' (King had replaced Clyde

McPhatter as the lead singer in the Drifters just before leaving the group for a solo career); 'Yakety Yak', 'Searchin'', 'Poison Ivy', 'One Kiss Led to Another' and 'Charlie Brown' for the Coasters; 'Kansas City' for Wilbert Harrison, 'Smokey Joe's Café' for the Robins, and 'Black Denim Trousers and Motorcycle Boots' for the Cheers. What a list of not-to-be-forgotten masterpieces. Pop Genius at work here!

THE BIGGEST OF THE BIG BAND ORCHESTRAS

In researching this book, I discovered that not only were writers and publishers well represented in the Brill Building, but at one time so were the most popular Big Bands of the Swing Era. I was intrigued because along with my family I had watched the Guy Lombardo Royal Canadians swing band's annual New Year's Eve television show—a must-see—for many years. He started the tradition on radio in 1928 and moved on to CBS television in 1956. Lombardo's first serious competition for this spot came in 1973 from *Dick Clark's New Year's Rockin' Eve*. As a preteen, I used to sneak down the stairs to my basement and peek in at my sister Marilyn's parties, where she and her friends would dance to the music of the Big Bands. Many of you will be too young to remember how big these Big Bands were, so let me tell you about four of the biggest of them.

Perhaps the biggest of the Big Bands was the Benny Goodman Orchestra. Goodman, a clarinetist, was called the King of Swing. His band was the first jazz band to play at Carnegie Hall and the concert was sold out, marking a leap forward for jazz bands. In fact, at the time, it was called "the single most important jazz concert in history". The concert introduced Goodman's 'Sing, Sing, Sing' which featured the drummer Gene Krupa, and became one of the biggest swing hits of all time. Even more importantly, Goodman was the first bandleader to put black musicians and white musicians together on stage despite the prejudices of the times (Lionel Hampton on vibraphone and Teddy Wilson on piano).

Glenn Miller was a trombonist. His Orchestra had more hit singles than any of the other big bands. Miller's band climbed all over the charts in the late '30s and early '40s with songs like 'Tuxedo Junction', 'In the Mood', 'Moonlight Serenade', 'Pennsylvania 6-5000' and 'Little Brown Jug'. According to Michael P. Zirpolo on the blog Swing & Beyond, the second floor of the Brill Building was originally an open expanse suitable for a restaurant or a nightclub. The Paradise Restaurant was the first to open there and the Miller band entertained the patrons on two occasions in 1938. On December 15, 1944, during the Second World War, Miller boarded a plane from England to France to arrange a show for the troops who had liberated Paris. The plane disappeared over the English Channel and the mystery of what happened to Miller remains unresolved to this day.

Jimmy Dorsey was a clarinetist and saxophonist, composer and leader of The Dorsey Brothers Orchestra until his brother Tommy went out on his own. The Jimmy Dorsey Orchestra's many major hits included 'So Rare', 'Maria Elena', and 'Green Eyes'.

Tommy Dorsey was a trombonist, known as the Sentimental Gentleman of Swing. His theme song was 'I'm Getting Sentimental Over You'. Tommy was the younger brother of bandleader Jimmy Dorsey. After he broke with his brother, he led his very own successful band, the Tommy Dorsey Orchestra, from the late 1930s into the 1950s. His biggest hit was 'I'll Never Smile Again'.

OUR TURF

There were two major restaurants off the lobby of the Brill Building, Jack Dempsey's and the Turf Restaurant. The general rule was that the older crowd of publishers ate at Dempsey's and the younger crowd of writers ate at the more moderately priced Turf.

I recall one incident in the Turf which makes me shudder. I was eating there on February 3, 1959 when someone rushed in to spread the news that there had been a horrible plane crash. The accident had taken the lives of three rock 'n' roll heroes: Buddy Holly, one of the major stars of the decade ('That'll Be The Day' which charted as high as #2, and his double-sided hit 'Peggy Sue' and 'Every Day'), the Big Bopper ('Chantilly Lace'), and Richie Valens ('La Bamba'). Suddenly the room emptied out, the writers all racing for their writing rooms to try to write the first hit song about pop music's great loss. I actually felt shame that day for the songwriting industry.

In 1971 Don Mclean wrote and recorded a sensitive, classic song inspired by the plane crash. The recording was almost 8:30

minutes long—very unusual for a pop record. In spite of that, it was a worldwide hit and went to #1 on *Billboard* magazine's charts in 1972, staying at that position for four weeks. From then on, the crash has been known by the title of McLean's song, 'The Day the Music Died'.

In a much lighter vein, I was eating at the Turf with Al Byron—my co-writer for 'Roses Are Red (My Love)', Bobby Vinton's smash 1962 hit; 'Something Blue' for Elvis; and my own recording of 'Happy Go Lucky Me'. Al happened to look amazingly like Buddy Holly. A young fellow came over to our table and politely asked "Mr. Holly" for an autograph. Al said, "I'm not Buddy Holly." The young boy started to tear up and tried again. I whispered, "Make the kid happy, Al. Just give him the autograph." However, Al, who could be obstinate, emphatically insisted, "I AM NOT BUDDY HOLLY!" The young autograph seeker started to cry and ran back to his mother. Now she walked over to our table. Heads started turning our way. "Excuse me, Mr. Holly. My son didn't mean to bother you and you would make him very happy if you would just sign an autograph for him." I repeated, very sotto voce, "C'mon, Al. Be a good guy. Give her the autograph." But peace would not prevail. Al insisted that he was not Buddy Holly. The woman, now frustrated and angry, said, or should I say shouted, "I will never again let another Buddy Holly record into our house." Al had done his best to ruin Holly's career.

I was back at the Turf one afternoon when Jack Keller, a good friend of mine who would become one of popular music's top writers and a songwriting hero of mine, saw me and sat down at my table. Jack would write a long list of hit songs, including Connie Francis' 1960 #1 hit song 'My Heart Has a Mind of its Own'. (The title provoked radio station WNEW's disc jockey, Lonny Starr, to introduce the record as "The song that astounded the medical field.") Jack had written 'Three O'Clock Thrill', one side of the Kalin Twins recording. I had written the other side, 'When'. (Oh yes. Once upon a time there were two sides to a music disk. Strange, but true.) So Jack and I made a bet on whose side would chart. Jack lost.

A few years later, with a few hits now under his belt, Jack told me about a secret method that he would sometimes employ to write a song. This is tricky, so strict attention please. Ready? Okay. Jack was sure that some hits followed certain patterns. So he would pick out a hit song that he admired and strip the lyrics from it. Then he'd write a new lyric to the song's melody. Finally, he'd strip away the original song's melody and write his own melody to it. Voilà. Jack had written a new song. Well, my song 'Roses Are Red (My Love)' was on the charts at the time, so I said, "Jack, don't you dare do that with 'Roses Are Red'." His answer was, "It's too late."

AND NOW I'D LIKE TO GET SOMETHING OFF MY CHEST

The Brill Building, the heart and soul of popular music, is located at 1619 Broadway. Many people called the area immediately surrounding it the New Tin Pan Alley. It was responsible for the beginnings of what came to be known as the Brill Building Sound, which got its name from the songs that tumbled out of the building in the late '50s and early '60s. So the Brill Building Sound became synonymous with the rock 'n' roll of that era. The building centered an area with many other buildings that housed music industry offices: record companies, writers, music copyists, publishers, orchestras and record producers. However, its address was 1619 Broadway, and I've always taken some pride from the fact that I was one of the first young singer/writers to show up at the Brill Building. But then Aldon Music hit town.

Donny Kirshner and Al Nevins formed Aldon in 1958. Nevins, a guitarist, was one of the founding members of the Three Suns, an instrumental trio that had been popular through the '40s and '50s. They were signed by RCA Victor in 1944 and their first record, 'Twilight Time', written by the band and Buck Ram, was an immediate hit. (Buck Ram later managed and produced the Platters. He produced 'Twilight Time' with the group, and they took the song back to the top of the charts in 1958.)

Kirshner had graduated from the Bronx High School of Science, as had Robert Cassotto aka Bobby Darin. The two friends eventually teamed up as writing partners and had some success writing commercials for local stores and businesses. Kirshner managed Darin for a while before they agreed to go their own ways, and for both of them, going their own way led to great careers. Bobby's singing career is legendary, and Donny was soon to become a legend in the music publishing business.

Kirshner's story begins with Aldon opening up for business at 1650 Broadway and ends with a list of great writers and great songs that helped the Brill Building Sound dominate the pop charts. Somewhere along the way Aldon's writers have become Brill Building writers in magazines, encyclopedias, television specials and even interviews with the writers themselves. Yes, the Brill Building Sound is the sound of rock 'n' roll of that era, and Aldon certainly can claim a large chunk of that sound. However, the Brill Building's address is 1619 Broadway. Aldon's offices were at 1650 Broadway, a block and a half and around the corner from the Brill. I can only think that there's some magic in the Brill Building's name and that somehow along the way, as Aldon's writers began to dominate the charts, the two buildings became one, diminishing *my* building's singular reputation and enhancing Aldon's—which, as history tells us, didn't need any enhancing. Okay, that's off my chest! It's a persistent but petty annoyance, but I feel better for having written it down on paper. Thank you for allowing the author to vent.

Two young men, Neil Sedaka and Howie Greenfield, walked into the brand-new Aldon offices looking for a publishing contract. They played 'Stupid Cupid' for Donny and Al. Donny took the writers to play their song for his friend, Connie Francis, and Aldon was off and running. The list of Aldon's most important writers and their songs is too, too long to list here, so I'll just mention a small portion of them along with the song's associated artists to refresh your memories.

From the team of Cynthia Weil and Barry Mann:

'Don't Know Much' —Linda Ronstadt & Aaron Neville
'Here You Come Again'—Dolly Parton
'You've Lost that Lovin' Feelin'' (written with Phil Spector)—The Righteous Brothers
'On Broadway' (written with Leiber and Stoller)—The Drifters
'My Soul and my Inspiration'—The Righteous Brothers

Looking back, it's flattering to recall something that I'd forgotten about until now: Barry Mann's first stab at recording as a solo artist in 1958. Barry chose two of my songs to record under the name Buddy Brooks: 'Dix-A-Billy' (co-written with Jack Reardon and Woody Harris, and released by LaVern Baker on the B-side of her smash hit 'I Cried a Tear') and 'They Could Be Wrong' (co-written with Jack Reardon and Dave Fleischhacker). In 1961 Barry had a smash hit under his own name with 'Who Put the Bomp', which he wrote with Gerry Goffin.

Barry was a friend of mine. I don't know why he and I never wrote a song together, but the music world can be happy that we didn't. Who knows, Barry might never have written with his partner and wife, Cynthia Weil, and the world would be missing out on some wonderful songs.

Then there are the songs of Carole King and Gerry Goffin, an *impossibly long* list to choose from:

'Will You Love Me Tomorrow'—The Shirelles and eventually Carole herself.
'(You Make Me Feel Like) A Natural Woman'—Aretha Franklin
'Up on the Roof'—The Drifters
'One Fine Day'—The Chiffons

Carole King on her own:

'You've Got a Friend'—James Taylor
'Beautiful'—Carole King
'So Far Away'—Carole King
'I Feel the Earth Move'—Carole King

Neil Sedaka and Howie Greenfield gave us:

'Oh! Carol'—Neil Sedaka
'Laughter in the Rain'—Neil Sedaka
'Stupid Cupid'—Connie Francis
'Breaking Up is Hard to Do'—Neil Sedaka
'Love Will Keep Us Together'—Captain & Tennille

Jack Keller and Howie Greenfield:

> 'Everybody's Somebody's Fool'—Connie Francis
> 'My Heart Has a Mind of its Own'—Connie Francis
> The theme song for *Bewitched*—Steve Lawrence
> The theme for *Gidget*—Johnny Tillotson

Donny Kirshner asked me up to his office once. It was very impressive. I remember deep carpeting, a beautiful grand piano and Donny's huge desk. He invited me to join his retinue of great writers. I was flattered, but I had heard how competitive the office was. When some artist asked for a new song from Aldon, Donny set teams against teams. That just wasn't for me.

Just how competitive was it? Well, one day I spotted my friend Barry Mann, certainly one of Aldon's top of the pyramid writers, running fast down the street. I managed to stop him and congratulate him. "What for?" he asked. I told him that I was congratulating him for having three songs in the Top 10. "Oh yeah," he answered, "but they're all on the way down the charts and I'm late for a demo session of a new song." And off he ran.

DEMONSTRATION RECORDS—SINGER FOR HIRE

I should mention here that I made a bit of money from co-writing 'When', but after being released from Atco Records I had to find some way to earn a steady income. I had sung on my own demonstration records, but it occurred to me that not all writers could sing. So I turned my attention to singing on other writer's demos. When news hit Tin Pan Alley that an Elvis Presley session was in the works and Hill & Range was looking for new songs, I knew that it was time to make my move. I loved rockabilly music and could sing it well. I could even sound a lot like Elvis. So I let it be known that I was available to sing for other writers. Not that I would make my fortune singing on demos; I believe that the going rate was $12.00 per song at the time.

My first stop was Associated Recording Studios, two blocks from the Brill Building at 723 Seventh Avenue. It was many a songwriter's choice as the studio where they would produce their

The Large Room at Associated Studios

demonstration records. Associated was owned by Nat Schnapf and Paul Friedberger, and it was a friendly place to hang your hat while you waited for the previous session to end. It was also a very busy place. I ran into Paul Simon, Tony Orlando, Johnny Rivers and Jerry Keller there. Jerry was a very popular demo singer and eventually had a great career as perhaps the Number 1 male jingle singer in New York. He also had a big pop hit with 'Here Comes Summer' in 1959. The song spent 13 weeks on the *Billboard* Top Hits chart, peaking at #14. Although the record never hit the Top 10 in America, it did reach the #1 spot on the UK's *New Musical Express* charts.

I got to know the engineers at Associated: Warren Schatz, who would later become head of A & R at RCA and produce Vicki Sue Robinson's smash, 'Turn the Beat Around'; Jerome Gasper who worked with Warren at RCA and then went on to Epic Records where he signed Luther Vandross, kicking off a successful R & B career for the artist; and Artie Friedman, who gained fame as a top engineer in the jingle business. Associated was a great training ground for young recording engineers.

Recording engineers were the most unappreciated group in the recording procedure. They were as important on the path to a hit song as were the musicians, singers and arrangers, because whether it was a demo or the final recording, they made the songs sound good. They were musicians—except that their instrument was the mixing board. They were the producers' partner in the studio and often helped them out when they hit a snag in the recording process. For instance, when I needed a "sound" for my demo of 'I Gotta Know', which I wanted played for Elvis Presley, another Associated Studio engineer, Larry Schnapf, suggested: "Shooby Dooby Da Da". Silly maybe, but it wound up on Elvis' recording of the song.

As important as they were to record making, sound engineers had no union protection. They contributed to the development of a hit record and then were no longer financially connected with it. I discussed this situation with some of the engineers who I was friendly with, urging them to try to get into the musicians' union, the AFM, so they could at least have some sort of a pension plan. It took until 2010, when the Nashville branch of the union finally agreed to allow sound engineers to join the union—a move too late for those engineers who were so helpful to me during my career. I believe the situation has changed generally for today's top studio engineers, who can demand and get credit for their part in the production and receive a piece of the record's money pie.

The Dick Charles Studio was another studio just up the street at 729 Seventh Avenue. Aldon Music monopolized the studio's time, although their writers did work occasionally at Associated. Aldon booked so much time at Dick Charles that after a while no one else would even bother to try to schedule time at the studio, and Dick Charles was forced to negotiate a lower rate with Aldon Music.

Associated Studios had two recording rooms: a large room, where you could fit a good size group of musicians; and a small room, where you could just fit a singer and his guitar. The large room was equipped with a vocal booth where you could isolate a soloist, to prevent "leakage" from the instruments into a soloist's track. One day, when I had just finished singing for someone in the large room, one of the engineers pointed me toward the small room. I went into it and discovered my friend Ira Howard recording a ukulele-playing, strange-looking man singing in a high falsetto voice with a crazy (I thought) vibrato. I must admit that I laughed at the scene along with the engineers at Associated—and, I'm told, so did Ira's bosses at Mills Music. Why was Ira wasting his time on this project?

Wasting his time? If you haven't guessed by now, the artist was Tiny Tim, best known for 'Tiptoe Through the Tulips' and for getting married to Miss Vicki on *The Tonight Show Starring Johnny Carson* on December 17, 1969, in front of an audience of upwards of 20 million. Unfortunately, but probably unsurprisingly, the marriage ended in divorce in 1977. Tiny was married twice more.

The *New York Times* wrote about the singer: Initially, journalists and critics debated whether Tiny Tim was a put-on or the real thing. It quickly became clear that he was genuine, a lonely outcast intoxicated by fame, a romantic in pursuit of a beautiful dream. "These voices," he told an interviewer, "really live within me."

I had a rewarding career as a demo singer and built up a pretty large clientele of important writers. I sang on three demos that were recorded by and became national hits for Carl Dobkins Jr.: 'My Heart is an Open Book', a #3 record for Carl, written by Hal David and Lee Pockriss; 'Lucky Devil', which reached the #25 spot, written by Aaron Schroeder and Wally Gold; and 'Exclusively Yours', Carl's third hit in a row, #62 on the national charts, written by Ben Raleigh and Don Wolf.

After I had my own hits, I stopped singing on other writer's demo records. Coincidentally, Carl's records stopped hitting the charts. One day I ran into Carl, and he begged me, jokingly of course, to please resume my demo career so he could get back to making hit records.

Chapter 2
WHEN PUBLISHERS RULED THE SONGWRITING WORLD

THE PUBLISHERS' SONS

At the same time that I was laying down vocals for other writers, I was showing my songs to publishers in the Brill Building. Some of them had finally come to the correct conclusion that there was no stopping rock 'n' roll. It was coming at them faster than a speeding bullet, more powerful than a locomotive, and able to leap the Brill Building in a single bound. Rock 'n' roll was the future of pop music publishing. Wisely, some publishers turned to their sons to sign up songs and songwriters for their firms.

For instance, George Wiener, who ran a very successful publishing firm, Wemar Music, held many standard songs in his catalogue, yet he put his son Stuart in charge of developing new talent and new songs. It wasn't long before Stuart's love of rock 'n' roll led Wemar to pick up the publishing of 1959's 'Shout', written and performed by the Isley Brothers. Stuart also co-wrote the lyrics for 'To The Aisle' with Billy Dawn Smith for the Five Satins in 1956. Also quartered in the Brill Building was George Pincus, originally a song plugger, and a very clever and perceptive independent publisher. He was one of the first independents to open an office in England, and sent one of his sons, Lee Pincus, an early Beatles fan, to London to run the office. Lee started making visits to Dick James Music, a publishing company that controlled some early Beatles' copyrights. Dick was apparently impressed that an American independent publisher had opened an office in London, so he made some sub-publishing deals with Lee, including one for the Beatles' 'She Loves You'. This obviously turned out to be very rewarding for George's pocketbook. He soon was headed to London and Dick James Music, where six deals were made for six Beatles copyrights, including 'From Me to You' and 'I Saw Her Standing There'. Sending a Beatles fan to run his office in England was one great move by George.

MILLS MUSIC

Mills Music was one of the first publishers to move their offices into the Brill Building in 1932. Jack Mills had founded the company in 1919. Before that, he was working as a song plugger for a music company. When he received a bonus of $500, he used it to set up his own company, Jack Mills Music, Inc. His younger brother Irving joined him as the Vice President and was responsible for signing new writers for the firm. The brothers caught a break when Enrico Caruso, the great opera singer, died. They were quick to purchase a song entitled 'They Needed a Songbird in Heaven, so God took Caruso Away'. The song was a hit and was followed by another huge success, 'Mr. Gallagher and Mr. Shean', which sold a million sheet music copies—and Mills Music was off and running. However, it turned out that 'Mr. Gallagher' was one of the last songs to sell millions of copies of sheet music; phonographs were now replacing pianos in American households. So by the early 1920s, the brothers moved into managing performers as well as supervising and arranging recording sessions.

In 1921 Mills Music added songs by two black songwriters to their catalog, which caught the attention of many other talented black composers who had great difficulty getting published up to that time. One of the first to join Mills was Jimmy McHugh, a pianist who had been working as a song plugger in Boston. (Song plugging seems to have been the entry into publishing for—well, for everyone?) Mills hired McHugh as a staff pianist and professional manager to help with promotion. McHugh was also a talented writer. He co-wrote 'I Can't Give You Anything but Love' with Dorothy Fields, the only woman to achieve songwriting success in the first half of the twentieth century, and the first woman to be elected into the Songwriters Hall of Fame.

Spoiling the story of the Mills brothers and their remarkable successes, *The Clipper*, a weekly publication for the entertainment business, reported in 1923 that composers placing songs with Mills Music were complaining about the "cutting in" of Irving Mills and Jimmy McHugh. Sometimes Mills and McHugh were listed as co-authors for making minor suggestions. That policy of sharing a piece of the writers' royalties has haunted the music publishing business right up to today. To be fair, though, not even a hint of that practice came up when Paul Parnes and I arrived at Mills Music in the Brill Building and began showing songs to Jack's son, Stanley Mills, where the stories of publishers' sons continue.

Paul Parnes and I were writing together when we started to show songs to Stanley, who had risen through the ranks at Mills Music and was by then Mill's General Professional Manager. In the age of rock 'n' roll, Stan was one of the best publishers of Easy Listening music—music that was relaxing, pleasant and never jarring to the ear. *Billboard* magazine had a separate Adult Contemporary chart (originally called the Easy Listening chart) for this genre of music, and Stan's songs were often on it. Parnes and I could write these songs well, and so we were often up at Stan's office on the 3rd floor of the Brill Building. In 1965 Stan picked up a record for us on Columbia Records: Ray Conniff's 'Happiness Is'. Although the record just managed to hit the lower end of the national pop charts, the song became a big moneymaker for Paul and me.

First, in 1966, Kent cigarettes bought the rights to 'Happiness Is' from Mills Music to use in TV commercials. At the time, there were rules in America governing cigarette commercials on radio and TV. Cigarette companies were still allowed to run commercials, but the ads were not allowed to equate smoking with feeling good. (Cigarette ads were totally banned from the broadcast media in 1971.) Here is the original chorus of the song, 'Happiness Is':

> Happiness Is, Happiness Is, Happiness Is
> Different things to different people
> That's what Happiness Is.

Thinking the song was popular enough to be easily recognized, Kent's advertising agency, Lennen & Newell, left the verses' structure alone, but rewrote the chorus. They played the melody wherever the song's lyric, "Happiness Is, Happiness Is, Happiness Is" had originally been sung, and added "The Taste of Kent" after each two-word phrase. Then they replaced "Different Things to Different people," with "More Taste, Fine Tobacco" and went back to melody for the commercial's last line. These changes avoided using the words "happiness" in connection with smoking, which would have violated the American rule.

Okay, hard to explain, complicated and tricky. However, it worked. Smokers wound up hearing what they wanted to believe; that happiness really *is* smoking a Kent. The commercial won a Clio, an annual award for excellence in advertising.

The commercial ran for three years and a few weeks with the price of licensing the song going up each year. The contract included the year that the campaign only ran for a couple of weeks while Lennen & Newell decided whether or not to renew. (They didn't.) What a bonanza for the writers and the publisher—a year's payment for less than a month's use.

Then, in 1973 Paul Parnes got a call from a friend who lived in Arizona with exciting news: the State Fair was using 'Happiness Is' as its theme. Paul and I put Mills Music to work. They wrote to Arizona that they expected to be paid for the use of their copyright. (I think they asked for $2,000.) Arizona didn't reply. The result was a lawsuit and a constitutional argument. At trial, Arizona argued that the Eleventh Amendment established that federal courts did not have the authority to hear cases brought by private citizens against states. However, the Court ruled against them and the judge ordered Arizona to pay for their sins. His order was ignored by the state until the judge started fining them daily. They wound up paying $75,000 plus $25,000 in court costs for something that could have cost them $2,000. Parnes and I split $37,500 and ran all the way to the bank. And it's a good thing that we did run, because eventually the Arizona courts' decision in our favor was held to be incorrect.

Of course, I've written a much-simplified layman's account of a very complex states rights issue. If you want the full account, type: *Mills vs Arizona, Happiness Is* into Google.

When the original Ray Conniff record was released, Stan, the "King of Easy Listening" (my name for him), got to work doing his "thing", promoting the song to other artists. He collected a ton of cover recordings. Here's a short list:

Count Basie with the Alan Copeland Singers
Herb Alpert & the Tijuana Brass
The Mariachi Brass
Hugo Winterhalter & His Orchestra
Clark Terry & Chico O'Farrill

Stan's assistant at Mills, Bernie Pollack, perhaps the last of the song pluggers whose job it was to get "live" performances, got the song onto TV, featuring on:

The Jimmy Dean Show
The Mike Douglas Show
The Lawrence Welk Show
The Danny Kaye Show
The King Family Show

In 1968, Hubert Humphrey, a Democrat, was running against Richard Nixon, the Republican nominee, for president of the United States. Mills Music was contacted by the Democratic Party for permission to use 'Happiness Is' for their campaign theme song. (They ultimately chose to use 'Happy Days Are Here Again', a song that was written by Milton Ager and Jack Yellen in 1929).

It boggled my mind when a very short time later, the Republican Party contacted Mills Music, requesting permission to use the song for *their* campaign. This had to be an unusual situation. But again, the request was withdrawn. So Paul and I wound up politically 0 for 2, but flattered that our song had both major political parties show an interest in it.

I have one more story about 'Happiness Is'. Paul Parnes and I were invited to Count Basie's recording session. We were both thrilled to be there, standing next to Joe Williams, "The Boss of the Blues", who had recorded what was probably one of my favorite blues songs, 'Alright, Okay, You Win', with the Count Basie Orchestra. That day, Parnes and I saw how admired the great Count was. It was amusing to hear the crowd of Basie fans literally swooning over any little mistake made by their hero. The recording of 'Happiness Is' was released in the album *Basie Swingin' Voices Singin'* with the Alan Copeland singers, and was released as a single that reached #28 on Billboard's Easy Listening chart.

SEPTEMBER MUSIC

In 1964, Mills Music was sold to Utilities and Industries Corporation. Stan, obviously a music pro, stayed with the new Mills Music until 1966, when he went to work at E. B. Marks. This created an interesting situation for him.

First, some background. The American Society of Composers, Authors and Publishers (ASCAP) was created in 1914 to license public performances and collect royalties for the writers. By the 1930s, radio had become increasingly important, and ASCAP tried to force large raises in its rates to broadcasters, threatening to pull its music off the air. The broadcasters retaliated by forming their own licensing agency, Broadcast Music, Inc. (BMI), and boycotting ASCAP songs. The war was on. At this point, the Justice Department of the United States stepped in and opened an investigation of all three parties: ASCAP, BMI and the broadcasters, for monopolistic practices. In 1941, to avoid litigation, ASCAP voluntarily offered broadcasters a better license and also cut ASCAP's fees to less than half of what it had been in 1940. In return, the broadcasters called off their boycott of ASCAP songs. The war was over.

Now, Mills Music had eschewed BMI songs despite Stan's protestations to his father, and E. B. Marks had made a deal with BMI, offering royalty money up front and letting it be known that the firm wasn't much interested in ASCAP songs. In his position as General Professional Manager, Stan overcame internal resistance to take songs from both ASCAP and BMI.

In 1968, Stanley formed his own companies, September Music (ASCAP) and Galahad Music (BMI) at 161 West 54 Street, another Tin Pan Alley building. Located there were Cy Coleman; Johnny Tillotson's management team of Mel Shane and Joe Sicorela; Tannen Music; music attorney Jules Kurz; Dan Aron's radio and TV production house, No Soap Radio; and my own office.

Although we didn't have any big hits at September Music, Stanley did deliver enough Adult Contemporary and Country charted records to keep Paul Parnes and me busy and happy. Here's a short list of some of my favorite songs published by September Music:

'Feelin'', recorded by Marilyn Maye, climbed to #14 and spent 18 weeks on the Adult Contemporary charts. The legendary Ms. Maye has been called the Queen of Cabaret, while Ella Fitzgerald praised her as one of her favorite singers—and "the greatest white female singer in the world". Getting her to record a pop sounding song like 'Feelin'' was a coup for September Music and Jim Fogelsong, who was in charge of her career at RCA Victor. Now into her 90s, she maintains a full schedule of appearances; see marilynmaye.com.

'Think Summer', recorded by Marilyn Maye and Ed Ames got to #17 on the Adult Contemporary (AC) chart. Ed, a former member of the famous Ames Brothers ('Naughty Lady of Shady Lane', 'You, You, You'), had his own solo career as an actor (the 1960s hit TV series *Daniel Boone*) and as a solo recording artist with hit songs such as 'My Cup Runneth Over' and 'Who Will Answer?'. 'Think Summer' was also recorded by Country Music's Roy Clark. His version hit the #20 spot on that AC chart. The Living Voices recorded it for RCA Camden, and I recorded the song for Laurie Records.

The Hillside Singers was a group put together by the ad agency McCann Erickson, strictly for a Coca-Cola ad called 'I'd Like to Teach the World to Sing'. The commercial was a big winner for Coke and the song was rerecorded by the Hillside Singers' and became their first hit record. Parnes and my song, 'The Last Happy Song', was recorded by the group and hit #22 on the AC chart.

'Congratulations, I Guess' was recorded by both Jerry Vale and Jane Morgan, although it didn't hit the charts. Jerry had a string of popular songs in the '50s and '60s including 'Two Purple Shadows' and 'Al Di Là'. He popularized some Italian songs like 'Innamorata' and was a hero in the Italian community. I was having lunch with him at a popular Italian restaurant when the owner recognized him and raced to put a Jerry Vale LP on over the restaurant's speaker system. Jane Morgan had a successful career in France before coming to America where she had a huge success with 'Fascination' on Kapp Records.

'If I had my Life to Live Over' was recorded by country music legend Slim Whitman, who was renowned for his yodeling and his unusually large falsetto range. He was even more popular in the UK than he was in America and in 1956 he became the first-ever country music singer to perform at the London Palladium. I recorded the song for Musicor Records in 1977.

HILL & RANGE MUSIC—WRITING FOR ELVIS PRESLEY

Perhaps the most important publishing company in the Brill Building was Julian and Jean Aberbach's publishing company, Hill & Range Music. It was noted for its great success in Nashville's country music industry and had an office located on the top floor of the Brill Building. The Aberbachs' cousin, Freddy Bienstock, ran their sub-company, Elvis Presley Music. The only way to get your songs to Elvis outside of Nashville was to play your song for Freddy and hope that he liked it well enough to tell you to make a demonstration recording that he would then send to Elvis' producers in Nashville.

So when New York songwriters heard that a Presley session was being planned, we'd write songs specifically for him, show the songs to Hill & Range and demo the songs that Freddy chose. We had to be careful to make our demos sound like an Elvis recording. The singer had to approximate Elvis's style, and the arrangement had to sound like an Elvis arrangement. I sang on my own demos and on demos for some other writers who couldn't sing like him. The final Elvis recording would often be just an improved version of the demo. I first noticed this when I mixed pieces of my original demo of 'I Gotta Know'—my first Elvis recording—with Elvis' version of the song on my recording equipment at home. The two versions were in the same key and at the same tempo. And when I finished mixing the two together, there it was: a Paul Evans/Elvis Presley duet for my personal collection.

However, there was one problem with writing songs for Elvis—and writers knew it. If Elvis Presley recorded your song, *one third of the writing royalties went to Elvis.* For the most part, I managed to duck that giveback by either not returning phone calls or by breaking appointments with Hill & Range when I knew that Elvis had

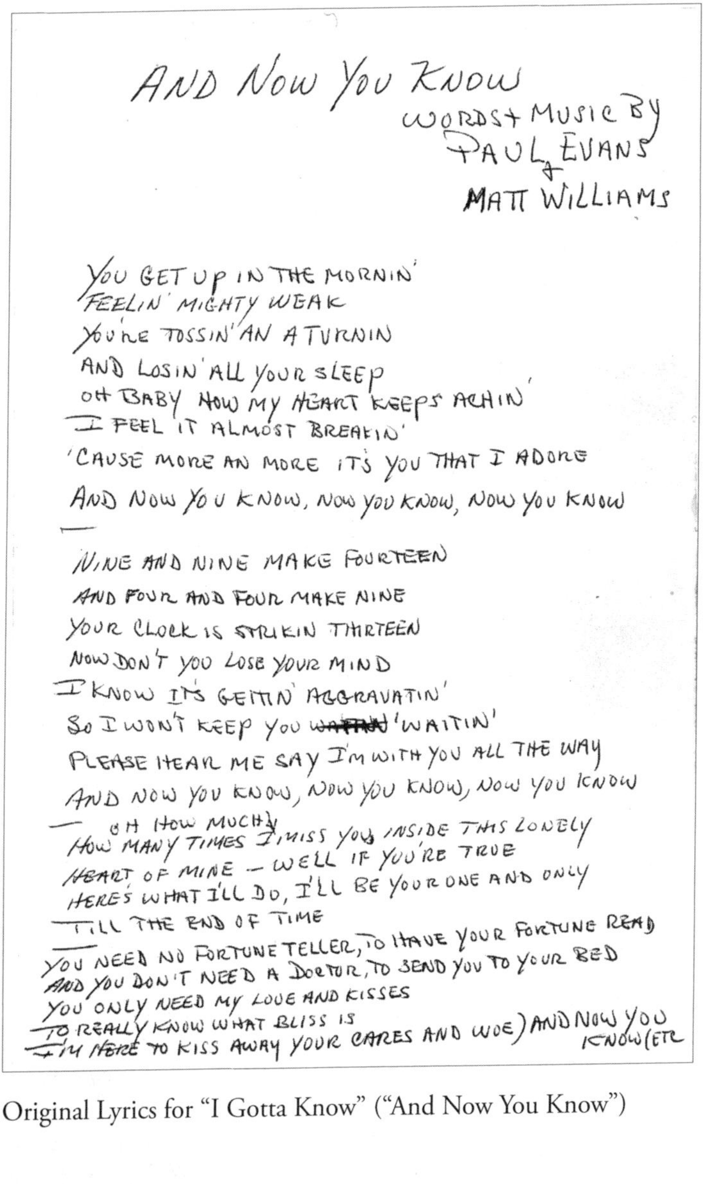

AND NOW YOU KNOW

WORDS + MUSIC BY
PAUL EVANS
+
MATT WILLIAMS

YOU GET UP IN THE MORNIN'
FEELIN' MIGHTY WEAK
YOU'RE TOSSIN' AN A TURNIN
AND LOSIN' ALL YOUR SLEEP
OH BABY HOW MY HEART KEEPS ACHIN'
I FEEL IT ALMOST BREAKIN'
'CAUSE MORE AN MORE IT'S YOU THAT I ADORE
AND NOW YOU KNOW, NOW YOU KNOW, NOW YOU KNOW

NINE AND NINE MAKE FOURTEEN
AND FOUR AND FOUR MAKE NINE
YOUR CLOCK IS STRIKIN THIRTEEN
NOW DON'T YOU LOSE YOUR MIND
I KNOW IT'S GETTIN' AGGRAVATIN'
SO I WON'T KEEP YOU ~~WAITIN~~ 'WAITIN'
PLEASE HEAR ME SAY I'M WITH YOU ALL THE WAY
AND NOW YOU KNOW, NOW YOU KNOW, NOW YOU KNOW

OH HOW MUCH
~~HOW MANY TIMES~~ I MISS YOU INSIDE THIS LONELY
HEART OF MINE – WELL IF YOU'RE TRUE
HERE'S WHAT I'LL DO, I'LL BE YOUR ONE AND ONLY
TILL THE END OF TIME

YOU NEED NO FORTUNE TELLER, TO HAVE YOUR FORTUNE READ
AND YOU DON'T NEED A DOCTOR, TO SEND YOU TO YOUR BED
YOU ONLY NEED MY LOVE AND KISSES
TO REALLY KNOW WHAT BLISS IS
I'M HERE TO KISS AWAY YOUR CARES AND WOE) AND NOW YOU KNOW (ETC

Original Lyrics for “I Gotta Know” (“And Now You Know”)

recorded one of my songs. I was finally cornered by their attorney, who shoved a paper in front of my nose when I showed up at their office. It was a blanket agreement, assigning one third of the writers' shares of songs cut by Elvis to Elvis. It had already been signed by a shockingly large group of successful New York City writers. "Kid," the attorney glared at me, "you can't duck this anymore. Sign on the dotted line or else forget about any more Presley recordings."

We went into Freddy Bienstock's office. "Freddie," I complained, "you promised that I wouldn't have to give up any of my writing credit or royalties to get Elvis." "I promised you that?" he asked. And when I swore that he had (and he had), he turned to the attorney and instructed him, "This man does not have to sign that agreement." Hill & Range eventually tore up that onerous agreement and I was very proud of myself when Freddie told me that my refusal to sign was partly responsible for the change in policy. I don't know what else might have inspired the reversal, but kudos to Freddy and Hill & Range for reversing their position on the Elvis cut-in.

Unfortunately, it is an age-old music business tradition for writers to trade some of their writing royalties with a singer or record producer who is hot and can therefore guarantee a successful record. As Spencer Leigh writes in *Buddy Holly: Learning the Game*, "Remember how Al Jolson's name appeared as co-writer on many songs? I'm sure the writers were happy to get a Jolson recording this way. Al Jolson would have said that he was the one making money for the writers." (Jolson was popular in the 1920s and '30s.) There are so many instances of this practice throughout popular music history that somehow it has become accepted business practice, and just something that songwriters have to cope with.

Presley recorded four of my songs. The first was 'I Gotta Know', a song that took a shadowy path to get to Elvis. It was scheduled to be recorded and released in Elvis's next album, *Elvis Is Back*, in 1960, but by mistake the song found its way into a package of songs sent to the Hill & Range London office to be shown to Cliff Richard. Cliff liked the song and recorded it for his own album, *Cliff Sings*, released in 1959. As a rule, Elvis would never cover another artist's recording. Any Elvis recording had to be the first time the song was ever heard, with the exception of a standard like 'Are You Lonesome

Tonight?'. But I got lucky. Freddy Bienstock managed to keep the Cliff Richard recording quiet and my song came out on a Presley single as a B-side to 'Are You Lonesome Tonight?'. 'I Gotta Know' peaked on the national charts in 1960 at #20. 'Are You Lonesome Tonight?' went to #1 in three weeks and stayed there for six weeks.

I wrote 'I Gotta Know' in 1959 with Matt Williams. We took our time with the lyric that we originally titled 'And Now You Know'. We knew that Elvis had recorded our song, but it had not been released yet. Then one day Freddy called me to a meeting at H & R. For some reason he asked me if I would like to have 'I Gotta Know' recorded by a new young singer that Freddy had a lot of faith in. But again, if this new singer recorded it, the Presley recording would never be released. It seemed like a simple answer: "No, no, no. I WANT ELVIS," I practically shouted at Freddy. Matt was furious with me for turning down an immediate recording for the possibility of a future Presley release—and even more upset when we discovered that the new young singer was Fabian, and we thought, incorrectly, that our song might have been on his first album. (We didn't know that the Fabian album had already been recorded and was "in the can"—the can that held the master tape.) However, once the Presley record was released, Matt was no longer angry with me. Unfortunately, he became overly enthusiastic about the money that he was sure he'd make on a Presley recording. I started hearing rumors that he quit his job at the Post Office and left his wife and family.

That news was particularly unfortunate because Matt and I were a good team. We had written a couple of songs besides 'I Gotta Know' (including 'Hushabye Little Guitar', a song that I would eventually record myself). However, we never wrote together again and, as a matter of fact, I lost track of Matt; our paths never crossed afterward. That was a very unusual situation for a team of writers who had scored an Elvis Presley recording.

The second song of mine that Elvis recorded was 'Something Blue'. It was released in the UK as the B-side of 'Kiss Me Quick', written by Doc Pomus and Mort Shuman. Unfortunately it was never released as a single in America. It was only released as an album cut in Elvis' *Pot Luck* album in 1962. What a shame. I believe it was one of the best lyrics by my co-writer, Al Byron:

Something borrowed was the heart I gave you.
You returned it torn in two
And that's why I'm Something Blue

Al was a terrific writer who provided the lyrics for another big hit for me. More about that song a little later.

'Blue River', my third Elvis recording, released in 1965, was not a favorite for either my co-writer, Fred Tobias, or me. However, I did get several fan letters proclaiming the song to be their favorite Presley recording. That's what makes popular music so unpredictable.

I wrote my fourth and last Elvis recording, 'The Next Step Is Love', with Paul Parnes (released in 1970), a song about young love in a complex world—and that's how I met my wife. I had gone through a rather difficult divorce and sworn off any more "entanglements". But only a few years later, Susan, a great-looking flight attendant, was in a café with a friend who found Elvis' recording on the jukebox. Her friend was dating a buddy of mine and knew that I had written the song. She played it for Susan and suggested that she should go out with me. "You'll like him and have a good time, but you won't fall in love." She was right. Susan liked me and we had a good time. But she was wrong. We did fall in love and still are, thanks to Susan's good friend and 'The Next Step Is Love'.

Elvis died on August 16, 1977. Hill & Range was holding two of my songs for him when he passed away: 'Quiet Desperation' (based on a line in *The Maine Woods* by Henry David Thoreau) and 'Tender Moments'. Both songs were co-written with Paul Parnes.

TANNEN MUSIC

When Country Music stars and music industry people like Chet Atkins came up to New York City from Nashville Tennessee, Tannen Music was always a first stop. That's because Nat Tannen, who founded the firm in 1944, was probably the only New York publisher who knew and respected country music at the time. Nat's son Paul joined the firm in 1960 and took over running it when his father died in 1962. Prior to 1960, Paul worked for Archie Bleyer's Cadence Records, promoting the label's artists like the Everly Brothers, the Chordettes and Johnny Tillotson.

When Tannen Music picked up the song 'True True Happiness' by Dick Wolf and Hal Greene, Paul pitched it to Archie Bleyer for the Chordettes. However, Bleyer, whose instincts were generally correct, decided to cut the song with Tillotson. Paul was soon managing Johnny's career and the two of them formed the Ridge Music Corporation specifically for songs that Johnny wrote. Ridge's biggest copyright was Johnny's 1962 big hit song 'It Keeps Right on A-Hurtin" which went to #8 on the *Billboard* Top Ten. By then, Johnny and Paul had become lifelong friends.

How did I fit into this twosome? While I was visiting radio station CKLW in Windsor, Ontario on a promotion tour for my own record, the two of them walked into the station while they were promoting one of Johnny's records, and we immediately clicked. The duo became the trio. I actually paced the hospital floor for Johnny when he was performing in Texas and his first wife gave birth to their son, John Michael. Johnny took a private plane back to New York but arrived too late and missed his opportunity to pace.

Ridge Music published and Johnny recorded many songs that I wrote with Paul Tannen, Paul Parnes, and Jack Reardon. Parnes' and my song 'There's a Fool Born Every Minute', recorded by Skeeter Davis, peaked at #16 on *Billboard's* Country charts in 1968, Reardon's and my song 'Worried Guy', recorded by Tillotson, peaked at #37 on the Hot 100 in 1964, and 'Our World', also recorded by Johnny Tillotson and written by Parnes and me, peaked at #70 in 1965.

Johnny eventually moved to California, where he lives with his wife, Nancy. We still get together whenever he's in the New York area for a performance.

Paul and I stayed in the New York area. I counted on him for music business advice and we spent many years hangin' out until I lost him on November 14, 2017.

PLANETARY MUSIC

Another Brill Building publishing office where I auditioned some songs was Planetary Music, run by Phil Kahl. However, I didn't realize that Phil had a partner, the notorious Morris (Moishe) Levy, owner of the famous Birdland nightclub and Roulette Records.

Fredric Dannen, in his music business exposé *Hit Men*, writes: "Morris' gangster ties were never a secret to the record business. His power came from copyrights. He understood early in the game that a hit song is an annuity, earning money year after year." And John Broven, in his book *Record Makers and Breakers: Voices of the Independent Rock 'n' Roll Pioneers*, tells of a Levy "smash and grab" with the 1960 Joe Jones New Orleans hit record 'You Talk Too Much', adding that the producer, Harold Battiste, was "scared to death" because "oh man, Phil Kahl and those cats—that's the Mafia!"

The Planetary office's atmosphere should have tipped me off that this was like no other publishing company. I was treated one day to the sight of a small group of tough-looking guys standing around in the office reception area, all with fedoras pulled down close to their eyes, making it hard to see their faces, and with "something" bulging under their jackets.

I liked Phil Kahl and thought that he liked me. He once introduced me to a couple of songwriters from Baltimore, Helene and Jack Polun, and asked me to finish up a song with them. I did, and Phil got us a recording of the song, 'Batch of Love', by Don Rondo, whose major hit record was 'White Silver Sands' in 1957. Unfortunately for the Poluns and for me, 'Batch of Love' never charted.

Phil stopped me one day in the office and asked what was bothering me. I told him that I had just lost my own writing room. "Not a problem, kid," he said, "you can use our writing room anytime you want to and you don't have to give us the songs you write." What a nice deal this seemed to be until a week later when Phil saw me. I was about to go into the writing room when he stopped me and asked, "Where are the songs, kid?" Whoops!

Nat Tarnopol had an office in the Planetary complex. He ran Brunswick Records, a subsidiary of Decca Records, and managed Brunswick's superstar Jackie Wilson ('Reet Petite', 'Lonely Teardrops' and many more). Once again, according to Fredric Dannen's book, "Tarnopol was a notorious abuser of artists. He had taken ruthless advantage of Jackie Wilson by designing contracts that left the singer perpetually in debt to Brunswick, even as his records made hundreds of thousands for the label."

I was walking past Nat's office one day when he called, "Hey, kid. Come in here. I want to talk to you." Now if Mr. Tarnopol told you he wanted you to come into his office—you went into his office. "Kid, I think I'd like to manage you." Wow, the manager of a major star thought that he'd like to manage me. "Because kid," he continued, "If I manage you, I'm going to make a *lot of money* and you'll *make [some] money too.*" The message was clear to me. My earnings were of no concern to him. I would have to say "no" to the offer—meaning I would never be able to step into that office again. Bummer. The office's good-looking receptionist and I had just started dating. We agreed that it was not a good time to continue seeing each other.

AL GALLICO MUSIC

One last word about music publishers. They all had strengths and weaknesses. Some of them had forged tight connections with record company executives, record producers or artists. Others could spot a good song when they heard it, and know immediately where they could take it to get it recorded. Al Gallico had strengths in both areas and offices in both Nashville and New York City. It was well known that Al had an eclectic ear. He published great country hits like 'Stand By Your Man' by Tammy Wynette and 'Almost Persuaded' by David Houston. But he also published 'House of the Rising Sun', recorded by the Animals, and the Zombies' 'Time of the Season'. His great relationships within the music community and his talent for matching songs with artists made him a very successful publisher.

Al had been a writer himself and was known around New York as a bit of a "song doctor". That meant, of course, that he would inspect the lyrics for a bad line in a song that he wanted the writers to make better. (Not a bad idea.) Al Byron and I wrote a song that we wanted to show to him, but we knew that he probably would dig deep to find something in the lyric to dispute. So we deliberately wrote a line that really wasn't in sync with the rest of the lyrics and brought the song to his office. Gallico went straight to that line and asked us to write a replacement while he went to take care of some other business. "Let me know when you've got something," he said, and then left us alone in his writer's room to write a better line. It was easy to do because Al and I had come prepared with a much better line. We just replaced the out-of-sync line with our original line, played it for Gallico, and he accepted the song and had us make a demo of it. We thought that we had played a funny gag on him. However, the joke was eventually on us because Al Gallico, successful publisher that he was, could never get us a recording of the song.

Chapter 3
STAR TIME

SEVEN LITTLE GIRLS SITTING IN THE BACK SEAT

I was still working as a singer on other writers' demos when I got a call from Associated Studios that Lee Pockriss and Bob Hilliard wanted to book me for a session. Lee had composed 1957's 'Catch a Falling Star' for Perry Como. Bob Hilliard was a bit older than Lee, having written 'The Coffee Song (They've Got An Awful Lot Of Coffee in Brazil)', recorded by Frank Sinatra in 1946. The song that I sang for them was a novelty song titled 'Seven Little Girls Sitting in the Back Seat'. They also booked two female singers, Sue Singleton and Susan Terry, both part of the Ray Charles Singers and regulars on Perry Como's weekly TV show.

The two writers took the demo right over to Joe Carlton's Carlton Records. They wanted him to cut the song with Merv Griffin, a nightclub singer who had scored a #1 hit with the novelty song 'I've Got a Lovely Bunch of Coconuts' in 1950. He hosted his own television game show, *Play Your Hunch*, in 1958 and was only a couple of years away from creating *Jeopardy*, probably the most successful game show in American television history—and still going strong.

Carlton told Lee and Bob that he had started a new label for more current artists and he would like to release the demo itself—as is, singers and all. The label was called Guaranteed Records and the girls and I would be called Paul Evans and the Curls. So back to the Associated Studios we all went to record the B-side of the record, Lee and Bob's song 'Worshipping an Idol'.

Promotion for 'Seven Little Girls'

'Seven Little Girls Sitting in the Back Seat' was released in August 1959 and was an immediate radio favorite. The record was originally scheduled to be released in September and I admit to just hanging around while I waited. One afternoon in August I was lying on my bed with my radio tuned to one of my favorite pop stations. I heard a familiar sounding song coming from the radio's speaker. Ever so slowly the song came into focus, until—*Yeowwie!* Then *Oh, my God!* It was 'Seven Little Girls', my record, playing on the radio. What an unexpected and terrific surprise. I called down to my mother and father, "Mom. Dad. Come listen to this. It's my record on the radio." They came, they heard, and I conquered—from doubts and disapproval to faces now showing their pleasure in hearing my record on the radio. All was well. My mother no longer had to struggle on the phone whenever her friends asked how her son was doing. I started spinning the radio dial immediately, and that afternoon and evening I heard my song eight times on the three New York pop stations.

To illustrate how hot the record was, WHK, a major Cleveland, Ohio pop station, made it their "pick hit of the week", which guaranteed the record one play an hour for seven days. Using my calculator, that came to 168 plays for the week. What a great start for my record. The song also inspired lots of silly radio station contests—i.e., "Why you would like to share a seat with the seven little girls?" and "Guess how many girls can squeeze into an average car's back seat". 'Seven Little Girls' wound up in the Top Ten on the *Billboard* charts but only got to #25 on the UK charts, beaten out by the Avons, an English group whose cover record hit the #3 position.

Unfortunately for Sue and Susan (the Curls), Joe Carlton decided that he didn't want the Curls on Guaranteed any more and he dropped them from the label. Everest Records quickly signed them, and to take advantage of their name being connected with a big hit record, released the first of two Curls records in November. However, neither of the two records caught fire and their recording career as the Curls was over.

Carlton was a seasoned music man. He had been a music editor at *Billboard* magazine and chief of A & R (Artists and Repertoire) for Columbia, Mercury and RCA Records before he formed his own label in 1957. Because he had high hopes for 'Seven Little Girls', he put a strong campaign behind it with respected promotion men Juggy Gayles, George Furness and Morris Diamond. Then the label sent me on a packaged tour that included, among others, Johnny Maestro & the Crests ('16 Candles'), Santo & Johnny ('Sleep Walk') and Bobby Comstock ('Tennessee Waltz'), whose band played backup for us. When I got on the bus, Bobby asked me what songs

I was going to perform on the tour. "Songs?" I was only prepared with one song—my hit, 'Seven Little Girls'. No one had bothered to let me know that I was expected to perform any more than that. However, Bobby was a pro and he asked me what kind of music I listened to. I told him that my love was folk music and he asked me to sing one for him. I chose 'Midnight Special', about a legend in a Houston, Texas jailhouse, suggesting that if the light of the Midnight Special train shone into your cell at the stroke of midnight, you'd be pardoned. The last line of the choruses was, "Let the Midnight Special shine it's ever-lovin' light on me." Bobby liked the song and we arranged it with a funky, rockin' beat. And that's how I wound up with a second song for the tour.

We were kids with hit records, and kids will play. So, to get onto the stage during the tour, I had to wrestle the drummer backstage and say "Uncle" before he'd let me go onstage to be introduced to the crowd. Yes, we were kids with hit records, and kids with hit records will be taken advantage of. Most of us were signed to the same talent agency. We were unaware that the agency, GAC, also packaged the tours. However, this created a problem for us. As our talent agent, they were supposed to get us the biggest fee they could get. But as a tour packager they wanted to book us at the lowest price that they could. What did they choose to do? Obviously they booked the artists at the lowest fee possible. I had the #6 record in the country and I was paid $400 for the week, and no expenses. And since the tour stops were spread out pretty far from each other, we had to sleep on the bus a few nights. I remember that GAC had us sleep over one night in a somewhat run-down and rather seedy single-unit motel. The practice of combining the talent agent with the packager was later found to be in restraint of trade and the agent/booker was put out of business by the government.

On this GAC tour, my first and last, the final stop was Bluefield, West Virginia. When the show ended, I got back on the bus and asked the driver how long it would take to drive back to our hotel. He told me that we weren't going back to the hotel; we were taking a 19-hour bus ride back to New York. No way! I had the driver drop me off at the hotel, called the airline the next morning and flew home (the flight cost me what I had been paid for my appearances that week). There would be no more packaged bus tours for me. I would go back to New York and get to work on my first album, *Paul Evans Sings The Fabulous Teens,* for Guaranteed Records.

Most of us teenage stars also had the same press agent working on our behalf. Connie DeNave had worked in publicity for ABC and as Dick Clark's press agent until she formed her own company, Image Makers. Some of her top clients were Frankie Avalon, Dion and the Belmonts, Fabian, and Bobby Rydell. She was a dynamo. I found myself in teenage magazines like *Teen Beat* and newspaper gossip columns, having incredible torrid affairs with female stars that I'd never met and being auditioned for TV and film roles that didn't exist. Here are a couple of examples of what I was supposedly up to—strictly for your amusement and bearing not an inkling of any resemblance to the truth (sadly, in some cases):

- Singer Paul Evans is singing to himself these days. Reason? Lovely showgirl Terry Hope. They're a steady duet at the Eden Roc.
- Joe Pasternak, who's made a career of discovering unknowns from Deanna Durbin to Paula Prentiss, is interested in singer Paul Evans who's interested in singer Micki Marlo.
- Perhaps you never heard of a singer named Paul Evans, but he has been creating such riots at personal appearances that his nervous managers have hired bodyguards for him.
- Singer Paul Evans, on the Coast after a Manila engagement in a triple play from Connie Francis to Yvette Mimieux to Cathy Carr.
- And my favorite: A columnist, commenting on our fictional romance, once called me "Connie Francis' favorite songwriter". Unfortunately, Connie never cut any of her favorite songwriter's songs.

I must mention that when 'Seven Little Girls' was released, it was banned in Boston. The reason? Boston, I was told, was a very Irish Catholic city and the powers that be distrusted the meaning of the lyric, "Keep your *snoopy* eyes on the road ahead". The ban sounds like it must have been a bad thing for my record since Boston had some very important rock 'n' roll radio stations. But it wasn't a bad thing, it was a good thing. In fact, when I heard that the record was banned in Boston I thought, "Looks like 'Seven Little

Girls' is going to be a solid hit." Why? The publicity value. Station programmers all over the country wanted to hear what it was that got the record banned.

TV LAND

I appeared on some television shows while my album was being readied. Dick Clark's Saturday night show was a "must": for my first appearance on *American Bandstand*, Dick had arranged for a mock-up of a car, with puppets playing the part of the girls in the back seat and a puppet that looked like Dick Clark as Fred, sitting in the back seat along with the girls. I "drove" the car. The show was broadcast from the Little Theater, off Broadway and just blocks from the Brill Building. To see a video of this, my first *Dick Clark* appearance, enter *Seven little girls paul evans, american bandstand* into your browser.

Throughout my career I performed seven times on Dick's Saturday night show. They were always fun to do. The audience was filled with young adoring fans who screamed, applauded and chewed gum. Occasionally the show would put up unique stage sets for the guest artists. When I performed my second Top 10 record, 'Happy Go Lucky Me', they dressed me in a Dutch Boy outfit for some reason and put me in a cuckoo clock set. Some of the audience were drafted, dressed in Dutch Girl outfits, and asked to chase me around the clock's revolving stage.

In his book, *Rock, Roll & Remember*, Dick mentions a performance of mine on his Dick Clark Beechnut show recorded outdoors in Philadelphia. I sat in a convertible car and Dick chose an unknown young man from the audience to play the part of Fred sitting in the back seat. That young man turned out to be Bobby Rydell, who was about to have a string of big hits starting with 'Wild One'. I guess you could say that I gave Bobby his start in show business.

Somehow, Dick's reputation was that of a businessman who was strictly interested in chasing profit, but you'd never guess that from my experiences with him. When I purchased my first video player (yes, *that* long ago), I got word to him that I would appreciate copies of my appearances on his Saturday night shows. Less than a week later, the tapes were hand delivered by a messenger. Then there was the time that I asked him for a quote for a compilation CD that

Susan and I were putting together. He faxed a flattering quote back to me almost immediately. And after I hadn't seen Dick for a decade or so, I was invited to a party at the Hard Rock Café in his honor. I walked over to him, prepared to reintroduce myself to him, but when he saw me, he quickly stuck out his hand and said, "Hello, Paul. Glad you could make it." Susan was with me and both of us were impressed with the warmth of his greeting.

In 1960 my co-writer Al Byron and I were asked to write a song for Merv Griffin's NBC show, *Saturday Prom*, which featured a live orchestra led by its bandleader, Bobby Vinton (who Al and I would write a major hit for in 1962). Merv asked us to write the "Name the Sandwich Song" for a contest, so we wrote, and I sang the 'Dum de Dum de Dum, Dum de Dum de Dum Sandwich Song' on the show. Its lyrics were filled with meats, vegetables and fruits, and the TV audience was asked to fill in the 'Dum de Dums' with a title for the song. Alas, I never did find out what our song wound up being named.

By far, the scariest television show I ever sang on was *The Arthur Murray Party*. Arthur and Katherine Murray owned a string of popular dance studios. They took advantage of the studio's name and turned it into a very popular network show, complete with the Arthur Murray dancers, singers and a full orchestra. The rehearsal went fine, except for the behavior of the chimpanzee that was to play Fred, sitting in the back seat of the convertible provided for my performance. This naughty little guy kept pushing his way into the ladies dressing room and gawking at the half-clad singers. The women also complained that he had a nasty habit of pulling up their skirts.

Okay. Showtime! I took my place in the car along with the chimp and the singers. My name was announced, the intro to my song began, the curtains began to part, and I panicked. I couldn't remember the first line of my song— which just happened to be the song's title, "Seven Little Girls Sitting in the Back Seat". I broke out in a sweat with perspiration pouring from my head. I was about to jump into entertainment's trash bin. But when the intro ended and the song began, I went on automatic and performed the song with no problems at all. It was nothing more than a close brush with disaster.

BACK INTO THE RECORDING STUDIOS

Because 'Seven Little Girls' was a bona fide Top 10 hit single, it was imperative to complete my album for Guaranteed Records quickly. This is a good time to tell you that young recording artists were at the beck and call of their labels because of the contracts that most of

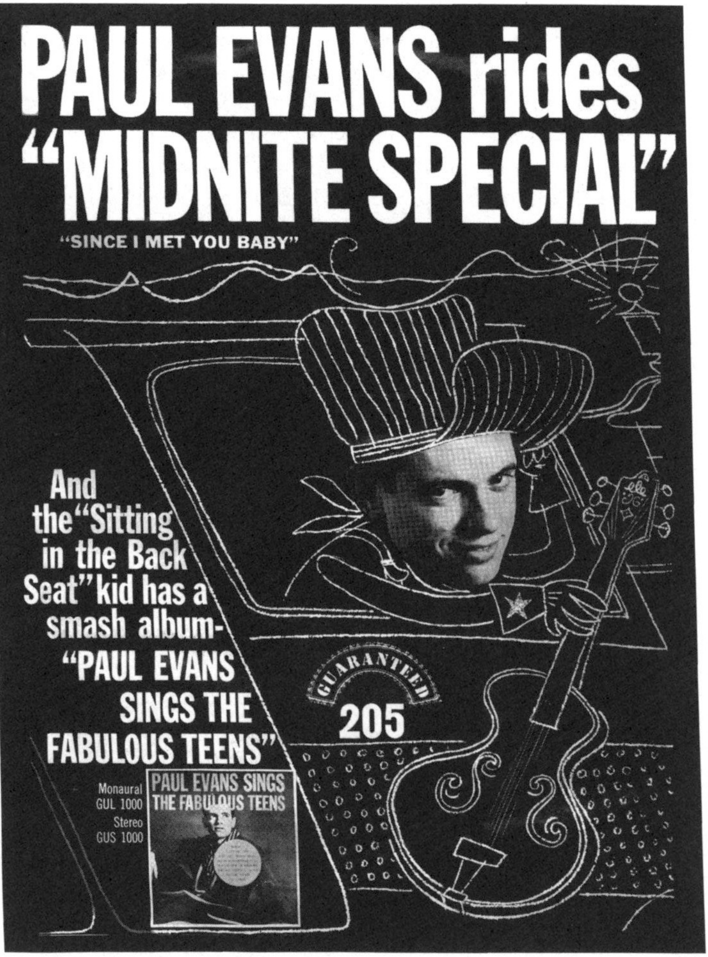

'Midnight Special' magazine promotion

us signed at that time. I could pick some of the songs that I wanted to record, but the label had the last word. We early rock 'n' rollers followed our lawyers into the record company offices at contract time. But as artists became aware of their power, they knew what they wanted, and *their* lawyers followed *them* into negotiations.

My first album would be filled with the hits of the day, but in an unusual move, would not include my current hit single. Don't ask me why. Ask Joe Carlton. Yes, he was the boss. However, I did manage to slip in 'Midnight Special', the song I had arranged with Bobby Comstock on that GAC tour, among the current hits.

I recorded the album, *Paul Evans Sings The Fabulous Teens*, in my comfort zone at Associated Studios. I used the same talented musicians I relied on whenever I had produced my demonstration recordings. New York City was filled with so many great studio musicians. My personal favorites were guitarists Al Gorgoni, Charley Macey, Bucky Pizzarelli and occasionally Vinnie Bell, probably the busiest studio guitarist in town. When Vinnie wasn't playing, Vinnie would be at home—inventing. He was one of the pioneers of electronic effects and would arrive at sessions toting his unique guitar and a boxful of pedals that would control sounds of his own design. I also worked with Dick Romoff or Russ Saunders on bass, Frank Owens or Leroy Glover at the piano, and Buddy Saltzman or Gary Chester on drums.

Whenever I think of those sessions, I smile at the thought of Buddy Saltzman. Buddy was one of the most sought-after session drummers during the 1950s, '60s and '70s. He was a fine musician as well as a fine drummer but was always ready to try something new. He found an old, unused electric heater at Associated and always kept it at the ready. 'Midnight Special' was the perfect opportunity for him to use the heater. He played a train rhythm on it with his brushes and that gave the recording the perfect feel. It's always been one of my favorite Paul Evans recordings and certainly the "funkiest" recording I ever made.

Guaranteed released 'Midnight Special' as my follow-up single to 'Seven Little Girls' and they turned on their publicity machine again. They sent me on a tour of record-hops around the country—local versions of the Dick Clark national dance party—and took full-page ads in *Billboard* and in *Cash Box* (another weekly music industry magazine with its own bestselling singles chart). Guaranteed got my picture on the cover *Cash Box*, waving from the cab of a locomotive to promote the song's train theme. But the record never really caught fire, and only managed to reach the #16 position on *Billboard's* charts. That would have been a respectable number except for the fact that it was the follow-up to 'Seven Little Girls', which had grabbed a spot in the Top 10. I'd have to do better the next time around—and I did.

However, I managed to get some delayed satisfaction from 'Midnight Special' when a few years later, during an interview with John Fogerty on the radio program *Shake, Rattle and Roll*, Fogerty was asked how he came to record 'Midnight Special' with Creedence Clearwater Revival. He said, "I remember hearing Paul Evans' version on the radio and it blew me away. I just added vibrato to my mix, rocked it up a little more and sang it the way Paul did." That took some of the sting from my having missed the Top 10. There were many versions of the song, but my recording was the highest charting version of it on the *Billboard* Top 100 chart. Johnny Rivers' recording got as high as #20 five years later. Creedence's version was only released in their blockbuster album *Willy and the Poor Boys*. Wilma Lee and Stoney Cooper had a wonderful version that hit #4 on *Billboard's* Country charts in 1959.

HAPPY GO LUCKY ME

My third release on Guaranteed was 'Happy Go Lucky Me'. It was a feel-good record that featured a maniacal laugh that I "borrowed" from a friend of mine. It put me back onto the Top 10, peaking at #10. And although it was not the smash hit I wanted, the song had a bright future. Years later, in 1998, 'Happy Go Lucky Me' was used as the theme for a new film by John Waters. He had previously written and directed the 1988 film *Hairspray*, an international success and later a hit Broadway musical. His new film, starring Christina Ricci and Edward Furlong, was about a photographer who finds fame in a world of pretentious artists. The name of the film was *Pecker*—because the photographer pecked at his food. Can you imagine what it was like being interviewed live on radio and asked the name of the film?

John Waters autograph—'To my Pecker Inspiration'

When Waters wanted 'Happy Go Lucky Me' as the opening theme for his film, he had to find my record. After all, it had been almost 40 years since the record had charted. His minions brought him a version that had been recorded for and released on K-Tel Records, an international budget label. However, he had great musical ears and said, "That's not the record that I remember. It's a cover record." He insisted that he wanted only my original hit recording of 'Happy Go Lucky Me'. So he sent his staff out again, and this time they searched harder and found the original.

By the way, Waters was a character and a difficult man to track down. I wanted an autographed picture of him, but no one could tell me where to direct my request. However, one day a friend of mine passed by a barbershop in Baltimore, the film-maker's hometown, and saw Waters sitting there. My friend walked in and asked if he'd autograph a publicity picture for me. Mr. Waters wrote, "To Paul Evans, my Pecker inspiration."

One more thought about John Waters. While promoting *Pecker* on national public radio, he said that he chose my recording of 'Happy-Go-Lucky Me' as the theme for the film because of its *"diabolical happiness"*. I thought that his description was right on target. Note: *Pecker* is R-rated. 'Happy-Go-Lucky Me' is not.

'Happy Go Lucky Me' was also used as an opening song on an episode of TV's blockbuster series *Scrubs* and was featured in Hulu's series *11.22.63*, based on a Stephen King novel about a man who travels into the past to try to prevent JFK's assassination.

And although George Formby's version of 'Happy Go Lucky Me' beat out my record on the English charts, I can't really complain. His version was used in a couple of TV commercials: for the video game *Clash of Clans* and a Christmas advert for the large UK supermarket Sainsbury's. And no matter whose version of a song is used in a commercial, the songwriters get paid for the song's use. 'Happy Go Lucky Me' has indeed been very, very good to me.

I had four more singles for Guaranteed. The first of the four to be released was 'Brigade of Broken Hearts', written by Fred Tobias ('Born Too Late' for the Poni-Tails and 'Good Timin'' for Jimmy Jones) and Clint Ballard ('Born Too Late' and 'You're No Good', taken to #1 by Linda Ronstadt in 1975). But the record could only manage to reach #81 on the national charts. However, I had high hopes that the next release, 'Hushabye Little Guitar', was going to bring me back onto the top of the charts.

Tony Wilkinson, who was known as "Wilk" to his many friends, was an *English* journalist who wrote a column for a *Swedish* magazine called *American Music*. The magazine published an extensive interview by Tony with me. His article began as follows:

It was 1960 and the scene was the local youth club monthly dance in Southend-on-Sea, Essex, England. The disc jockey announced that the evening was drawing to an end and it was time for a dance to hold your partner close. The regulars smiled knowingly as they knew this spot as "bum-grabbing time". Soon the hall was filled with couples tightly gripping each other as they staggeringly navigated their way around the floor in this quaint English version of dirty dancing. The music being played was Paul Evans' 'Hushabye Little Guitar', a local cult favourite and still a personal choice to this very day.

Unfortunately, bum-grabbing time was as far as the record got.

THRILLA IN MANILA

In April of 1961, I spent four days performing at the Araneta Coliseum in the Philippines with Johnny Preston ('Running Bear') and Pilita Corrales, a popular Filipino singer, songwriter, actress and television personality. My manager, Milt Schnapf, and I got the star treatment from the moment our flight landed in Manila. An airport representative came aboard the plane and announced our names. While the rest of the passengers waited, we were given leis and escorted off the plane. The first thing that I saw were fans—*my* fans—on the terminal's rooftop screaming my name and waving signs that read: "Welcome to the Philippines Paul Evans". The next thing I noticed was the red carpet that had been rolled out for me. Milt and I walked onto the carpet and into the terminal, where a crowd of photographers greeted us.

Then we were off to the Coliseum and a greeting area where we could catch our breath. I noticed two people playing chess and asked if I could play a game. I lost that game in five or six moves. How was I to know that chess was the most popular pastime in the Philippines? It wasn't long before I was whisked off to some radio stations to do interviews and promote the show. At one of the stations I met a tall, shy young man who was known as the Paul Evans of the Philippines. He sang only Paul Evans songs at his appearances. American music was the rage at the time and no doubt I wasn't the only American singer to have a namesake in the Philippines.

Arriving at the Araneta Coliseum

One night I was at a local club when the crowd found out that I was performing at the Coliseum. They insisted that I get up and sing something for them. Well, there was an awful lot of beer being drunk, and quite a bit of it by me. It wasn't long before the audience discovered that I could yodel. That provoked a lot of whoopin' and a-hollerin' and a night full of yodelin'. Mea culpa; my performance the next evening was not one of my best.

The Coliseum was located just outside of the capital city, and Manila was a very rough town and a very poor one. If the Araneta Coliseum's owner, Mr. Araneta, wasn't the richest man in the Philippines, he was certainly in the top one percent. He lived on the Coliseum grounds, his estate surrounded by barbed wire fencing. I actually saw a tank on his property. The entire crew that was involved with that week's Coliseum performances was invited to a party. Mr. Araneta's son gave us a tour of the grounds and took us to their huge garage, where we all stared at their collection of the world's greatest and most expensive cars.

Milt and I were warned to stay out of Manila; it was too dangerous. The eating and drinking establishments displayed signs that read: "Leave your guns at the door", and very violent teenage gangs created havoc in the streets. However, we convinced our Araneta guardians to allow our Filipino driver, Jorge, to take us on a day tour through the quietest neighborhoods if we would have him check back in with them every once in a while. When it was time for him to call in, he asked us if we had a dime to use a pay phone. He didn't even own a dime to make that call. Jorge asked me if I could leave my jeans behind for him when I left for home, which of course I did. This good man had a job—but no money.

The three of us went to have a lunch at the official American restaurant. As we walked to the door, the doorman pointed at Jorge and told us that he couldn't come in. "This restaurant is for Americans only," he told us. So I replied that in that case we would go elsewhere. After a brief discussion, they agreed to welcome us all in—I guess because they knew that I was starring at the Araneta and they wanted the "star" to eat there. When I got home, I received a note from our Coliseum escort telling me that Jorge said, "When Paul and Milt here, everything happy-happy. Now Paul and Milt are gone. No more happy-happy."

In the meantime, Milt and I had decided to go home by way of Japan and to take a little R & R there. One evening Milt disappeared and when I awoke the next morning, the money that I'd received for the gig at the Araneta, all in American dollars, was gone. When Milt returned, he admitted that he had used the money for his own recreation and defended his actions. After all, he said, he wasn't just my manager; we were also friends. Maybe, but now we were friends without money. Milt had to call his brother and ask him to wire funds so we could get back home. The incident was the beginning of a major rift.

SEPARATIONS

In 1959, Bobby Darin had had a huge #1 hit with 'Mack The Knife', which propelled him to superstardom. Bobby's rise was probably inevitable; he was a people magnet. I remember hanging out in the B&G diner on the ground floor of 1650 Broadway with a group of writers, chatting on a cold New York winter's day. I was talking with Gerry Granahan ('No Chemise, Please') when suddenly the door opened and all conversation stopped. All eyes turned to Bobby, who had stepped into the diner, flung his scarf around his neck and just stood there for few seconds. His entrance was like a charge of electricity, touching everyone.

'Mack The Knife' was a change from his very successful rock 'n' roll past and had fast-started his "cool", finger-snapping adult

Joe Carlton and me during the good times

image. That song, so adult, led to a great nightclub career and to many major television appearances. There's no doubt that Bobby Darin's success had record labels looking to lead their young rock 'n' rollers in the same direction and Joe Carlton was no exception. He was looking for the song that would take my image away from rock 'n' roll.

Joe received a phone call from the office of Bullets Durgom and Ray Katz. They asked him to let me know that they'd like me to come out to California, all expenses paid, and meet them at the Beverly Hills Hotel pool. Durgom and Katz wanted to speak to me? They managed several top acts, including Jackie Gleason. Perhaps Joe could have his next Bobby Darin. Joe and I could only imagine what Durgom and Katz could do for my career. So off I went to Los Angeles—only to face disappointment.

I went to the pool at the correct time and there they were. I remember two rather large men smoking cigars. After I introduced myself, they turned away from me and toward each other. Without another look at me and without asking me any questions, they started to talk about me and to discuss how they would take charge of my future career. Their conversation went something like 'First we'll send him to … He'll have to change his … We can introduce him to … He'll travel to … He'll take lessons from … etc., etc." No, this kind of a totally controlling artist-management relation wasn't something that I could ever live with. So back I came to New York City and my unsatisfactory situation with Milt.

Joe Carlton was angry with Guaranteed's distributors and decided to move my future recordings to Guaranteed Record's parent company, Carlton Records. Distribution was not an area I understood at all. However, I was aware of how important the distributors were to getting the records into stores and to promoting them. It might have been that the distributors were angry about the heavy-handed way that Joe handled the move from Guaranteed to Carlton Records. Or perhaps my records just weren't good enough. But the move to Carlton records marked the very end of that period of hit recordings for me.

Joe released two albums of mine on Carlton Records simultaneously in 1961. *Hear Him In Your Home Tonight* featured 'Seven Little Girls Sitting in the Back Seat' and 'Happy Go Lucky Me' and included 10 more songs that I had recorded, some released and some new. The other album was *Folk Songs of Many Lands*. I remember arguing with the Carlton team about the lyrics in 'Passing Through', a song written by Dick Blakeslee while he was attending college. The argument was whether or not the lyrics "Yankee, Russian, white or tan, Lord, a man is just a man. We're all brothers and we're only passing through "were too controversial to be released in my album. Controversial? Really? Too bad! This was one of the few times that I spoke back to the Carlton execs and I insisted that the song stay in the album, lyrics intact. The year was 1961. It would be nice to think that the world has gotten wiser since then.

Joe released four singles of mine on Carlton. The second was 'After The Hurricane'. Al Byron and I had written and recorded the demo and brought it up to Hill and Range, hoping that it would be approved for Elvis Presley. Freddy Bienstock approved it, but Milton Schnapf, who had been advising Al and me at the time, insisted that we should save it for my own record and not go forward with the Presley project. Okay. We all make mistakes in life, but that was a *huge* mistake. My demo was a hard driving rocker and the song would have made a great record for Elvis. My record did come out to terrific reviews, but Carlton was having problems by then and just could not get 'Hurricane' enough radio play. It was perhaps just too late to save my faltering recording career. My relationship with Carlton lasted for two more records, and Joe Carlton and I then parted ways.

I was disappointed with the royalties I had been paid for the couple of years that I had been with Guaranteed/Carlton, so I asked my attorney, Bill Krasilovsky, to look over Joe's financial books. Unfortunately Bill found over $40,000 in 1961 dollars that were never paid to me. Imagine my anger and disappointment. I had respected Joe as a mentor and as my record career "daddy". Why, I had even performed at Joe's son's Bar Mitzvah as a favor to him. Krasilovsky advised me that if I sued the label, it would go out of business. So the best I could look forward to was to getting the rights to my masters back.

Meanwhile, Milt and I continued to fuss. I finally got his attention and reminded him that nothing was happening. My writing and singing career was at a standstill and we weren't making any money together. I asked him to agree that our handshake management agreement should be discontinued. Before I could take a breath he answered, "No." He wouldn't even discuss the situation. He just said, "No." I felt like a jerk, sticking to a handshake agreement that Milt wouldn't even talk about. Well, it wasn't long before I realized that if he wouldn't talk about it, I'd have to settle it by myself. We were both obviously unhappy with the relationship and so I thanked him for what he tried to do for me, wished him luck (which he didn't even acknowledge) and told him that as far as I was concerned our agreement was over. He didn't seem to care, so I figured that having no manager was better than the nonproductive and contentious relationship we were in. I moved on.

BACK IN TIN PAN ALLEY'S ARMS

I must say that many, many record companies believed that I could get back on the charts with the right song. In fact, I have always thought that I might hold the record for the number of labels, excluding compilation labels, that any singer had records released on. Let's count them:

1. 1957 RCA VICTOR
2. 1958 DECCA
3. 1959 ATCO
4. 1959 GUARANTEED
5. 1961 CARLTON
6. 1962 KAPP
7. 1964 EPIC
8. 1968 COLUMBIA
9. 1971 LAURIE
10. 1972 RANWOOD
11. 1973 DOT
12. 1974 MERCURY
13. 1975 BIG TREE RECORDS
14. 1977 MUSICOR
15. 1978 SPRING
16. 1980 CINNAMON
17. 1993 GARDEN OF EDEN
18. 2006 FSA

Dave Kapp was a very respected and successful music man. He signed me to Kapp Records soon after I left Carlton. When I met him, he told me that the reason I hadn't had any successes after 'Happy Go Lucky Me' was that I could sing so many genres of music. He said, "We'll have to find the correct niche for you and stick to it." And then what happened? Dave released six Paul Evans' singles. Novelties, pop ballads, teen-oriented songs and finally, maybe out of frustration, a Country album, *Twenty-One Years in a Tennessee Jail* aka *Another Town, Another Jail.*

Chapter 4
UPS AND DOWNS

ROSES ARE RED (MY LOVE)

One day in 1962 Al Byron walked into Associated Studio A while I was making demos of some of my songs. He was holding a handwritten lyric in his hand, and put it on the piano stand. I took a quick look at it and jokingly told the musicians to "Take a five. I'm going to write a hit song now." I started to sing a melody to Al's lyric, 'Roses Are Red (My Love)' and Al said, "That's good." I spent a few months trying to improve on the melody I had written as a joke that day in the studio, but I couldn't do better. It just flowed. So I demoed the song, and because I had just left Kapp Records, I brought it to Bob Morgan, a producer at Epic Records, convinced that it would be a great song for me to record with him.

Bob loved the song but said that he had someone else in mind to record it: Guy Mitchell, whose recording of 'Singing the Blues' had spent 10 weeks at #1 in 1956. However, Guy's management wanted the publishing rights, and I wouldn't give it to them, so they turned the song down. Lucky for all of us, the turndown didn't diminish Morgan's determination to cut the song with one of his artists. He had a talented musician/singer on his roster, Bobby Vinton, who had one more recording session guaranteed in his contract with Epic, and Bob apologetically told me he would record the song with him rather than with me. Morgan later told me that he recorded 'Roses' twice with Bobby. And in an interview with Fred Bronson in *The Billboard Book of Number 1 Hits*, Vinton says that the first time he recorded it, it was recorded as an R & B song, "and the worst sounding thing you ever heard." The second recording was the winner, recorded closer to my original demo with strings and a chorus added—a little bit country and a little bit pop.

I can't say that I wasn't terribly disappointed that Morgan didn't cut it with me. However, Bobby Vinton's recording of 'Roses Are Red (My Love)' shot to #1 on the pop charts (Epic Records' first #1 record) and stayed there for four weeks. I was no longer disappointed. Al and I had our #1 record and the bragging rights that went with it. 'Roses' was proof that sometimes you work on a song for months until you have what you consider the world's first perfect song—but no one else likes it. At other times, as in this case, you write a song once through, try and try to make it better, finally give up and go back to your first instinct—and you wind up with a major hit. Go figure.

A lot of the credit for the success of 'Roses Are Red' belongs to Vinton. Epic Records originally promoted the other side of the record, 'You and I', a #1 hit in 1941 for the writer Meredith Willson. But Bobby was convinced that 'Roses Are Red' was going to be a big record for him. He was born in Canonsburg, PA, just several miles from Pittsburgh, and was a local favorite. So he sent a pretty model to deliver a copy of the record along with one red rose to every popular music station in Pittsburgh. His promotion worked and the record took off in Pittsburgh. Epic Records immediately turned their attention to 'Roses' and put a big campaign behind it.

I brought 'Life Goes On', a song that I wrote with Paul Parnes, to Bob Morgan, hoping that I could catch Vinton's next single. I sang it at the piano for Morgan, who immediately called Bobby, who happened to be in town, and asked him to come right over to his office at Epic. When Bobby came in, we were introduced, and he asked me to play my song for him. I did, and he said that he liked it and asked me to play it again. I was encouraged. So I played it again and Bobby said that it was a really good song. Now I was enthused. He insisted that I play it a third time. When I finished, Bobby said, "Paul, that's a Top 10 song." All right! 'Life Goes On' was a shoo-in for his next release. However, he added "But it's not a Number 1 song. I'm going to have to pass on it." What a mind twister. I've got to admit that I was hurt and angry with Bobby. He had raised my spirits and expectations and then brought me

My Manager, Milton Schnapf, with *Folk Songs of Many Lands*

down—hard. However, Bobby apparently knew what he was talking about. After 'Roses Are Red', he scored three more #1 songs on *Billboard*, and landed another five in the Top 10. My hat's off to you, Bobby Vinton. I must mention that Bobby did eventually cut 'Life Goes On'. It was released on his album *Mr. Lonely*.

Al Byron and I were generally aware that our copyrights were important. Unfortunately, we slipped up with 'Roses Are Red'. When Vinton's record was released, Milton Schnapf was still my manager and co-owner of my publishing company, Lyle Music, Inc., and Al and I still thought highly of how he handled business. When it was time to sign contracts, we told him that we wanted an AGAC contract, which safeguarded writers' future copyright renewals.

(AGAC is the American Guild of Authors and Composers.) Milt just smiled and said, "Don't worry, boys. When it's time for renewals I'll take care of it." And so we didn't worry. Take heed, young writers; because when Milt and I drifted apart, we agreed to sell Lyle Music to United Artist Publishing, which was eventually gobbled up by EMI Music. Milt's promise to "take care of it" was forgotten about by the three of us, and Al and I woke up one day to the fact that EMI now owned the worldwide renewals for our #1 song.

Luckily, our attorney, M. William Krasilovsky, who wrote *This Business of Music*, one of the bibles of the music business, was rummaging around in his attic one day when he came across the original contract with an attached letter that guaranteed that no matter how the contract read, American rights would be returned to the writers after the original term of copyright. He sent the required notice to the EMI attorney, informing him that we would be claiming the renewal for America. But the attorney wrote back that we had signed a white standard contract and therefore EMI owned the renewal. Bill called the EMI attorney and asked if he hadn't noticed the attached letter. Grossly, the attorney said, "Oh, you found the letter". When Bill complained about the ethics of holding back the truth, the attorney sneered that he worked for EMI and his job was to protect them, *no matter what*.

The fact that an EMI attorney would act in a way that hurt their writers came as no real shock to Al and me. Later, when I visited my English friend and sub-publisher Eddie Levy, and complained about how poorly EMI was paying us for royalties outside America, Eddie checked and found that EMI hadn't registered the song correctly in many of their territories around the world and that the lost royalties were gone forever. Al and I spent a long time trying to recover the lost royalties and talking with attorneys, trying to get our copyright back from such careless guardians, but those royalties really were gone forever.

And here's the kicker. Our attorneys in America and in England told us that if our original contract had been signed in England, we would have recovered our copyright. England's copyright law demanded that if you owned a copyright, you had to take care of it. But the contract was signed in America, where the copyright owner can wipe any part of his or her anatomy with it. Writers, guard your copyrights!

I discovered while reading the newspaper one day that Warner Brothers would be releasing *Goodfellas* in 1990, starring Robert De Niro, Joe Pesci and Ray Liotta, and directed by Martin Scorsese. It was going to be an important film. I also read that it would feature 'Roses Are Red (My Love)'. It so happened that 1990 was the year that Al Byron and I would get the American rights back to the song in America. We checked and found out that EMI had illegitimately signed the license for its use the year before, in 1989. That meant that any contract for the use of our song in the film had to be between Warner Brothers and us. So we called Warner Brothers Entertainment and announced that they'd have to deal with us, that their contract with EMI was null and void. We put Bill Krasilovsky on the case.

Warners' people asked if we would please abide by the deal that EMI had made for the song's inclusion in *Goodfellas*. Fat chance. EMI had contracted out the song at a very low price. Our song would be featured in an important scene at the Copacabana nightclub, with Bobby Vinton's own son acting the part of Bobby singing 'Roses' on the Copa's stage. Warner Brothers threatened that if "that kid" (me) didn't agree with their terms, the song would "wind up on the cutting room floor". Sure it would—not. Can you imagine Warner's telling Martin Scorsese and Robert De Niro that their film would be held up and that they'd have to reshoot some scenes because "some kid" was correctly negotiating a new contract for the song. We finally agreed to a fair price for our feature performance and also negotiated a royalty for any and all *Goodfellas*' DVDs sold. The DVD was a Top 10 seller for many, many years. This time, EMI's carelessness served Al and me well.

COVER RECORDS

Cover records are releases that come after the initial recording of a song is released—and a hit record usually generates many, many covers. That was definitely the case with 'Roses Are Red (My Love)' as it was with 'When', my Kalin Twins hit of 1958. The foreign response to 'When', my first hit record, was a wonderful surprise for me. I remember getting 30 or more covers from Europe alone. However, 'Roses are Red' was a blockbuster hit, #1 for four weeks, and so covers poured in, many from major artists here at home as well as around the world. A lot of the domestic covers were included in albums filled with current hit songs, but internationally, many of the cover records were singles by artists that hoped to hit their own country's charts—and sometimes did.

It wasn't just my hit songs that got covered; many of my songs that just managed to make the bottom of the charts here at home were covered abroad, and I especially looked forward to hearing those recordings. It was always fun to hear different interpretations of my songs, as well as copies of the original records' arrangements. And many of my songs have been covered around the world. I've heard my songs come back to me in Chinese, Croatian, Czech, Danish, Finish, French, German, Italian, Malaysian, Portuguese, Spanish, Swedish—and who knows what else? Some foreign lyricists would write as close an interpretation as they could of the original lyric, but that was sometimes impossible, given the differences in languages. In that case, the writer would come up with a brand-new lyric.

Here are some of my songs that were covered by major artists around the world:

Johnny Hallyday covered 'Our World' as 'Si Tout Change'. French lyrics by Jacques Chaumelle

Eddy Mitchell and Les Chaussettes Noires covered 'I Gotta Know' as 'Je T'Aime Trop', French lyrics by E. Mitchell and J. Dambrois

Eddy Mitchell covered 'Something Blue' as 'C'est à Nous'. French lyrics by Eddy Mitchell and Ray Brent

The James Brothers covered 'When' as 'Wenn'. German lyrics by Blecher and May

Gerd Böttcher covered 'Johnny Will' as 'Geld Wie Heu'. German lyrics by Hans Bradtke

Caterina Valente covered 'Roses Are Red' as 'Rosen Sind Rot'. German lyrics by Hans Bradtke

Kikki Danielsson covered 'Forget Me Not' in English Lyrics by Al Byron

George Formby covered 'Happy Go Lucky Me' in English Lyrics by Al Byron and Paul Evans

See Appendix, *Paul's Songs Recorded by Other Artists*

In 1971 I was at Midem, the leading international music event held yearly in Cannes, France. Hans Bradtke, a prominent German lyricist (see 'Geld Wie Heu' and 'Rosen Sind Rot' above) walked up to me and introduced himself: "Hi. I'm your co-writer." It took me a minute to figure out what he meant, but once I understood, we had a good laugh and became very good friends, managing to meet in Berlin and New York City a few times.

Of course, cover records go both ways between Europe and America. Bryan Wells and I wrote the English lyrics to 'When Love Is Gone', the theme for the film *Bilitis*, with music by Francis Lai. And I recently came across the blog "ABBA Blog #10: For Old Time's Sake, Man!". The story it told (and which I had forgotten) was that before Agnetha Fältskog, Björn Ulvaeus, Benny Andersson, and Anni-Frid Lyngstad became ABBA, they had a hit record, 'Hej gamle man!' ('Hey, Old Man!'). Björn and Benny wrote the song, and the blog said that in a 1972 interview, they mentioned that "some country guy" in America had recorded it. Turns out that I was that "country guy". Stanley Mills (September Music) had procured the American rights from the group's publisher, Stig Anderson, and Stan asked Paul Parnes and me to write the English lyric. We did, and I recorded 'For Old Time's Sake' for Laurie Records in 1971. Of course, at the time I had no idea who Benny and Björn were or how important they were going to be. And although my record wasn't a hit, the blogger, Carl Magnus Palm, an ABBA historian, says that as far as he can tell it does have a definite claim to historical fame. It's the earliest recording of an Andersson/Ulvaeus song by an American or British artist:

'For Old Time's Sake' by Ulvaeus, Anderson, Evans, Parnes

Imagine: ABBA's songwriting team and Paul Evans and his writing partner together in one credit. Ain't that something!

GET OUT OF THEIR WAY

1964 was a turnaround year for me. It was the year of the British Invasion, led by the Beatles, and the beginning of the end of Tin Pan Alley's and America's stranglehold on popular music. The Beatles might have led the charge, but right behind them in that first wave of British groups came the Rolling Stones, the Kinks, the Dave Clark Five, the Animals, and the Hollies. And they just kept coming and coming and overwhelmingly filling the American charts. On April 4, the Beatles held the top five positions on *Billboard's* Hot 100 with their singles 'Can't Buy Me Love', 'Twist and Shout', "She Loves You', 'I Want To Hold Your Hand' and 'Please Please Me'. They then broke Elvis Presley's record of nine singles on *Billboard's* Hot 100 at the same time by scoring *fourteen* spots on the Hot 100 on April 11th. And let's not forget the British women who started to appear on the American charts during the Invasion: Dusty Springfield, Helen Shapiro, Marianne Faithfull and Petula Clark. I think the only established American acts that managed to cut through the British hold on the American charts were probably Bob Dylan, the Beach Boys, the Supremes and Simon & Garfunkel.

Petula Clark is a good example of the chanteuses' assault on the American Hot 100. She was born in 1932 and had been a star in England since the age of 10, singing on the BBC during the Second World War, and appearing in films since the age of 13. She had been a recording star in England since 1954 when she had her first Top 10 hit, and racked up hits in France, where she became that country's top female singer in 1962. She recorded in four languages, selling a million copies of 'Monsieur' in Germany. Petula was truly an international star, but still unknown to audiences in America. And when did we learn of her? It wasn't until 1965, when she became an "overnight sensation" with her recording of 'Downtown'. Her brilliant career here in the States continued with 'My Love', 'I know a Place', and 'Don't Sleep in the Subway', all written by Tony Hatch, the last one with his co-writer Jackie Trent.

I saw the writing on my wall. The safe and solid world of the Brill Building and Tin Pan Alley, where I was so comfortable, was collapsing. I would continue to write and record, but I was not in the center of the pop music world anymore. I'd better find some other source of income while I waited for the English artists to go away. Well, I always was a bit of a dreamer.

Chapter 5
SELLING KETCHUP

THE BIG, WIDE, WONDERFUL WORLD OF ADVERTISING

After 'Happiness Is' was accepted for the Kent cigarette campaign in 1966, I was asked to come up to Lennen & Newell, Kent's advertising agency. The music producer asked me if I knew the details of the recording by the Ray Charles Singers. He wanted the commercial to sound similar to the Conniff record, so he asked me how many singers there were, how big an orchestra Conniff used, and anything else that I could tell him about the session. Unfortunately, I wasn't present at the recording and couldn't provide him with any answers. But he taught me something. I learned that the singers on the commercial would earn more money than I made as the writer that first year. Well, I had written some hit songs, sung on demonstration recordings for myself and for other writers, and of course sung on my records. Why not take a shot at the big, wide, wonderful world of advertising?

At another ad agency—Batten, Barton, Durstine & Osborne—John Bergen and Phil Dusenberry had heard the Kent cigarette jingle, 'Happiness Is', and liked it. They asked me if I was a music producer as well as a writer and singer, and I said "yes". That was a little fib, as I had only produced my own demonstration recordings with a rhythm section and perhaps a few singers. I would soon have a reason to regret that little fib.

Bergen and Dusenberry asked me to produce an instrumental session for a major automobile company. Okay, I would begin my life in commercials as a producer. I assumed that I'd be asked to put the session together. *Never assume!* BBDO chose the music writer who also arranged for and booked a 20-some-odd piece orchestra and hired a huge recording studio. Uh-oh. We immediately ran into a problem at the session, which I couldn't solve. All agency eyes were on me and I panicked. I knew I'd be exposed as a fraud, that word would spread around the advertising community and that I'd never work in commercials again. So I told the BBDO attendees that I had to step out for a few minutes to clear my head. I really wasn't sure that I wouldn't go through the door, down the steps, and out into the streets—never to return again. But I stopped at the studio's phone and called my good friend, Paul Tannen, who had lots of experience recording large orchestras. He told me to calm down and asked if I knew the sound engineer. I did know him, so Paul told me to tell the man the truth. He added that he would come right over to the studio. So I walked back in and whispered into the engineer's ear that no matter what I told him to do, he was to ignore me and do whatever he thought was correct. I added, of course, that I would "take good care of him". Soon Paul Tannen burst into the room, and between him and the engineer the problem was solved and somehow I became a musical hero at BBDO. It was a wonderful example of learning on the job.

It wasn't long before the agency called me in to write and produce an ad for Pepsi Cola. It was a holiday weekend campaign. I wrote 'This Big Weekend Pair Up With Pepsi'. I hired an up-and-coming singer, Arlene Martell, to sing a duet with me for the commercial. The commercial was a success and I had chosen my singing partner well. Arlene developed into probably the most sought-after jingle singer in New York City, nicknamed "the Queen of Jingles".

I did lots of work for BBDO for several years. One of the less successful ones stands out in my mind. It wasn't just another Pepsi commercial; it was meant to be a long-running Pepsi campaign called "The Smiling Majority", a parody title of the Moral Majority, founded by Jerry Falwell and a conservative Christian movement that strongly opposed abortion, gay rights, the woman's rights movement and the Equal Rights Amendment. Everyone at the agency was well aware of how the title "The Smiling Majority" came about.

I made a recording for the Pepsi campaign with eight studio singers. Then BBDO had me record Delaney & Bonnie, a popular folk duet of the late '60s and early '70s. The agency also flew me up to Montreal to record the New Christy Minstrels, a hot 60s folk-rock group who had a major hit with 'Green Green'. The agency even had beach towels printed with the slogan "The Smiling Majority".

This was an expensive beginning to what was to be a major campaign. That is, it was until BBDO decided to test it in front of a focus group (a sample audience). Apparently a few people remarked that the title reminded them of the Moral Majority. And now the issue that BBDO knew about all the time threw the agency into a frenzy, and—bam!—the entire campaign was scrubbed. Okay, win some, lose some. (Actually, I didn't think that it was really okay. Too much effort, energy, time and money had been poured down the drain on what seemed, in retrospect, like a whim that was predestined to wind up badly.)

However, this wasn't a particularly unique situation in the advertising world. One of the first ads that I sang solo on was for a Chrysler car. It was scheduled to debut on TV on a certain program at a specific time and station, so I decided to throw a party. I invited a roomful of friends and family to celebrate hearing my voice on my first national TV commercial. Finally the time came and we all gathered around my television set and then … I shrank when an older Chrysler car commercial aired instead of my commercial. Was I humiliated? Oh yes, I was, and there was no way that I could pretend otherwise. The story that I later heard was that a Mercury executive met a Chrysler executive on a golf course one day and thanked the Chrysler man for advertising a Mercury car: "You showed a cougar [the animal] in your commercial, and I appreciate your advertising our Mercury Cougar brand." The Chrysler ad that I had sung on was scrapped.

Then there was the "Tropic Surf" debacle. Pepsi added a new citrus product to its line of soft drinks, and I won the competition to produce a jingle to accompany the product's initial release. All was going along so well. My music was accepted and recorded, and the commercials were ready to run, when … Susan and I had a carton of Tropic Surf delivered to our door. I opened the carton and took out a bottle. The label graphics were beautiful and very cool.

It made us think of Beach Boys music on a sandy beach. I removed the bottle top and poured us both a glass so we could toast to my new music campaign. And then, our first taste of Tropic Surf. *Yuck! Horrible!* And the public agreed. Tropic Surf had a short life span and my jingle never ran.

As I relive my jingle production history, I'm beginning to feel that all the time I spent looking for that one major campaign, I had a devil sitting on my shoulders. Okay, it's true that you win some and you lose some, but come on!

But wait. There's more. I knew of a major agency's executive who had the final word on what music would be accepted for the product. He had a unique way of making his decision. He played the music for his mother, and her opinion would be his guiding light. And then there was a copywriter friend of mine who was asked to come up with a name for a new product. Well, he'd always wanted to go to Japan, so he gave the product a Japanese-sounding name, the client accepted the name, and my friend got to go to the filming of the commercial in Japan (his suggestion).

But for all the trivialities and inanities sometimes displayed at advertising agencies, it was a very serious business with a lot of money at stake. If the commercial was meant for television there were film costs: actors, directors, sometimes a big star as a spokesperson, expensive time to be bought at TV stations, musicians, singers, arrangers and studios to be paid. And always present in the back of agency personnel's minds, a disastrous campaign could cost the agency its client, which would often be accompanied by the people who worked on the product being put out onto the sidewalk.

Besides the disappointments, there were those feel-good moments when the music supervisor at an agency respected you well enough to choose you to produce music for them without any competition. Such was the case for me when the agency for Esso and Enco gasoline chose me to produce the music for their big radio and television campaign introducing their new additive that prevented "hesitation":

Esso (Enco) Gasoline has HTA.
A couple of tanks will get you on your way.
It's a funny little put down, when you put your foot down.
And that's what hesitation's all about.

Paul's parents, Leah and Nathan

Paul with sisters Marilyn and Estelle

A local TV 'Hop'

In Your Home Tonight! album cover

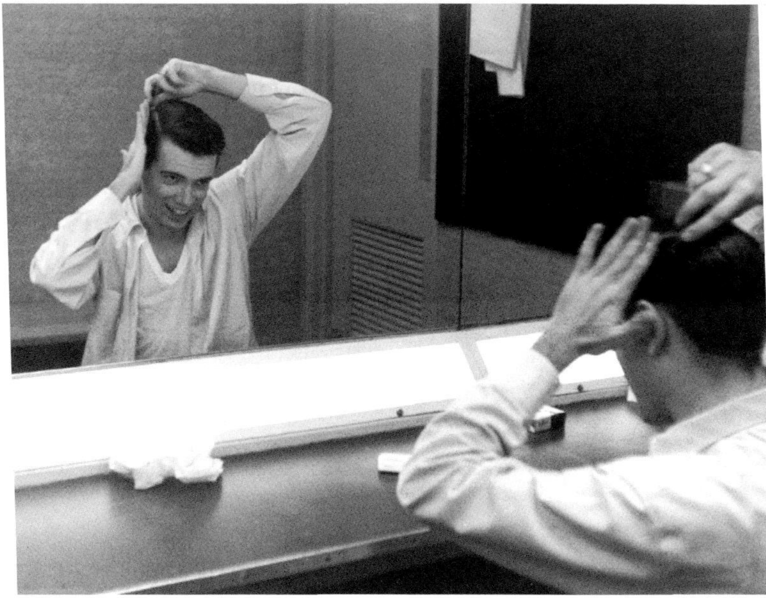

Dick Clark Show – getting ready

Dick Clark's Saturday Night Beechnut Show

Seven Little Girls – sheet music

Happy Go Lucky Me – sheet music

I Gotta Know – sheet music

When – sheet music

1959 – Seven Little Girls – double page *Cash Box* advert

1960 – Happy Go Lucky Me advert

Paul with songwriter, Cy Coben, and Chet Atkins

Paul – 1961

1961 – in the Philippines with Johnny Preston

Paul with his wife Susan in a recording studio

Paul and Paul Parnes receiving ASCAP Awards in Nashbville

Paul with WHN's Ed Salamon and rocker Robert Gordon

1979 – Paul with Donny Osmond at the Royal Albert Hall

Hello, This is Joannie – UK single cover

Joannie publicity pic

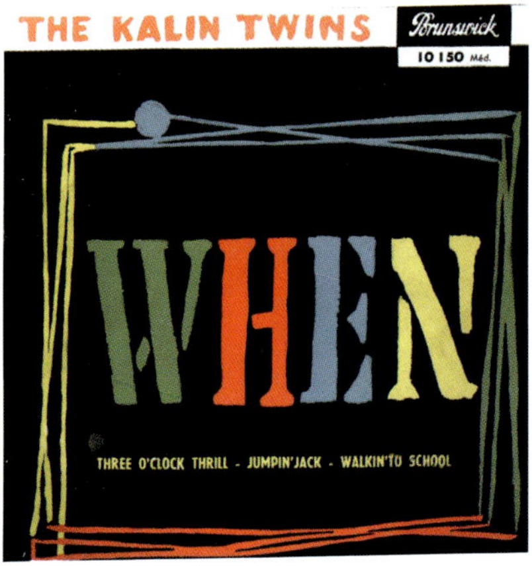

When EP cover

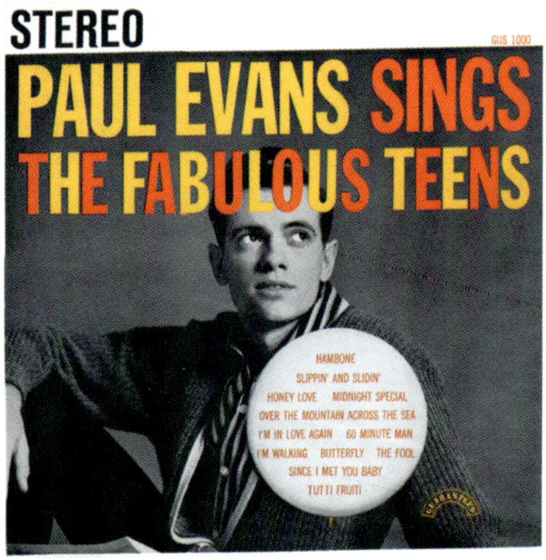

Fabulous Teens album cover

Folk Songs of Many Lands
album cover

Hello This Is... Paul Evans
album cover

Paul – in Nashville

Behind the board – © John Krondes

Back to the beginning – The Brill Building

I also produced the 'Your Old Friend Has a New Name' jingle when the names Enco and Esso were brought under the same name, Exxon.

The name change, by the way, led to one of my favorite corporate public relations faux pas. The Humble Oil Corporation had a problem. Because of a court ruling, they had to use two different names for their gasoline stations in different states in the United States, Esso and Enco. (We had to cut two versions of every spot we recorded for the "Hesitation" commercials, one for each name.) This created a problem for the oil giant. After intense research they decided on the name "Exxon" for all of their gas stations. Imagine their embarrassment when they discovered that the word Exxon is similar in pronunciation to the Japanese slang word for "stalled car". Heads must have rolled.

JINGLES ALL THE WAY

While I'm on the subject of commercials, many of our music stars got their starts singing on jingles: Barry Manilow, Randy Newman, Melissa Manchester, Michael Bolton, Patti Austin, Luther Vandross, and Valerie Simpson of Ashford & Simpson, just to name a few. I came at my jingle career the other way around. Hit record singer to jingle singer. Studio work was generally a very well-paying profession under the protection of the radio and television unions, AFTRA and SAG (the American Federation of Television and Radio Artists and the Screen Actors Guild). In 2012 the two merged into one union, SAG-AFTRA.

However, not all jingles are equal. Rates depend on which media the commercial runs on: public broadcasting, public service announcements (PSAs), cable, local, or network radio or television. Yes, it's a complicated formula and many people have the wrong idea about it. Jingles earn residual payments for the performers. Residual income is, simply put, the amount of money you get paid after your initial work is done. Generally, singers get paid for the original session and after that, there can be payments based on how often and where the commercial is played. Somehow, the word "residual" has become part of the public's lexicon. I can't count how many times I've told people that I sing on jingles and the comeback is, "Oh, then you make residuals. You must make lots of money." After hearing this too often, I lost the energy it took to explain to them that not all jingles are equal.

I was called for a jingle session for Ford, the giant American automobile company. The producer's regular singing group was called, and a new female singer (let's call her "Joan") was invited to join us. The producer had met her while she was singing at some social affair and asked her if she'd like to sing on jingles. Of course she would! Her first session was for a commercial that would air on national network TV, the juiciest category on the union books. We sang one jingle that would earn residuals based on its use in several national commercials—the pot of gold at the end of the jingle rainbow. We all earned a session fee for our one-day's work plus a large residual check based on future network play. Joan thought that she had stumbled into a little piece of heaven.

The next date for the producer that Joan sang on was for a small grocery store in the American Midwest. We all received checks for somewhere around $125.00—the session fee. So Joan, not being acquainted with how singers are paid for jingle work, called me and wanted to know when we'd get paid "the rest of the money". Sorry, Joan, but local spots just don't pay the same as network spots. However, as I explained before, it's a complicated system, so rather than try to explain it to her myself, I sent her up to speak to my go-to-guy, Bob Spiro, the singer's rep at AFTRA who would attempt to take the mystery out of the collective bargaining agreement between the unions and the American Association of Advertising Agencies for her. (Not an easy task.)

I was originally called only for solo work, a lot of it country and pop. However, I was missing out on group work, so I took lessons on sight singing (reading notes on a musical chart) from the fabled Helen Hobbs Jordan. Ms. Jordan taught sight singing for more than 50 years to aspiring singers and musicians as well as established stars who just wanted to polish up their knowledge of how music works. She was a strict teacher who just wouldn't abide mistakes from her students during classes. Her lessons provided me with a path to much more group work on jingles.

Every jingle producer worked differently with his or her singers. Jingle singers had to have a good "ear" for music because, for the most part, singers would come to the sessions knowing what product they would be singing for, but they had no idea of what type of music they would be asked to sing. Some producers would just sing the melody for the soloist to memorize and then ask the group to make up the harmonies once the soloist had recorded his or her part. If there were no soloist involved, some producers would have the group gather around a piano and hand out notes that he wanted the individual singers to sing. But no matter how the singers learned their parts, since we were being recorded on high-capacity tapes, or directly into a computer, it became standard practice to have all the singers sing the same note, then play the track back to them while they all sang another note on another track (this was called "overdubbing"), stacking tracks on top of each other until the producer was happy with the sound of the group. This method made the groups sound very, very large.

At this point, you might ask why I bothered to study sight-reading. The answer is that there were arrangers, sometimes the producers themselves, who knew exactly what notes they wanted the singers to sing and would place music charts with the words and notes printed on them in front of the singers. If you couldn't read music, you obviously couldn't work for those arrangers, and there were quite a few of them. One exception to this singers' rule was Jerry Keller. That's because Jerry had an incredible ability to listen to any melody just once and memorize it immediately. Once, on a jingle session, Jerry asked me, very sotto voce, to sing him his rather complicated part that was written down on the music chart in front of us. I sang it for him and he said, "Thank you", and didn't need to hear it again. I don't think that I ever met anyone else who could do that.

I have one more thought about commercials—about two that I refused to work on. During the Vietnam war I sang the solo on an Army recruitment jingle. When I got home, I had second thoughts about what I had done. I thought about my nephews, who were of enlistment age. They certainly had a right to join the armed forces if they wished to do so, but I felt that I shouldn't be influencing them one way or another. So when the jingle house called me to sing on another recruitment ad, I begged off, telling the music producer why I felt the way I did. He told me that the office understood and had encountered the negative response before. However, I never got another call from that jingle house.

Another time I was called into an advertising agency and asked to take part in a competition to write and produce the music for a cat food commercial. I was handed a lyric sheet to write the music for and went home to study the lyrics and start the creative juices flowing. I took a hard look at the lyric sheet and then another. Then I asked Susan to read what was written on the sheet of paper and to let me know if she agreed with me. She did. This ad wasn't selling food for your cat; it was meant as a cheaper meal for poor and elderly people who couldn't afford their food bills. Well, someone else could sell cat food for needy people. I wouldn't. (We had just seen a TV exposé about how pet food was being marketed to the poor and the elderly population.)

If the product had been for what I was told it was for, I certainly wouldn't have been too proud to write and sing for cat food—or toilet paper—or, for that matter, laxatives. Uncomfortable or not, if you worked in the advertising business, that's just what you did. A fellow jingle singer told me that one day he got home from a session and his young son asked him what he had done that day. "I sang about ketchup," the singer told his son. His son replied, "Silly daddy."

Chapter 6
SING, SING, SING

SOCIAL SERVICES

Whenever America faces a social or political problem, artists of all kinds are asked to contribute their services to cheer up the nation. In 1968, during the Vietnam War, many artists were asked to perform for the Americans fighting there. ASCAP, the songwriters' organization, asked me to join a group for a USO (United Service Organizations) tour of hospitals in the Far East, including Vietnam. I would join Harry Woods, who wrote a roomful of hits including 'Try a Little Tenderness'; Johnny Marks who would go down in history as the man who wrote 'Rudolph, the Red-Nosed Reindeer'; and Ranny Sinclair, a terrific singer who was added so we would have at least one pretty girl to perform for the soldiers who were far from home.

We got as far as Clark Air Force Base in the Philippines. When we got off the plane we heard loudspeakers cranking out orders to various flight crews to get into position and for others to take flight. I asked the Colonel assigned to us if this was a normal day at the base. Of course, what I was really thinking was: *Is there something going on that we should be concerned about?* He told me that every day, China sent aircraft towards Clark—and every day, American fighter planes were scrambled and ordered into the air to meet them. The Chinese would turn back at the last moment. He also told me that mistakes were sometimes made and one side or the other would lose a pilot and a fighter plane. "They're constantly probing our defenses," he added.

We entertained at a USO club on the base and at an on-base hospital, where I got a taste of the reality of war. I saw helicopters landing on the grounds of the hospital, stretcher-bearers racing to them, picking up the wounded and then racing back to the hospital. And I do mean "racing". It seemed that every minute counted. Some of the soldiers I met had been seriously burned by America's own phosphorus bombs that had gone off-course. Others had lost an arm or a leg to the war. Sadly, some of the injured had joined the army just to get the dental work done that they couldn't afford to have taken care of at home. And still others told me that they'd intentionally injured themselves because the army's policy at the time was "three injuries and out".

I think our little group helped. Ranny had to sing her way through whistles and comments that only the injured could get away with. Johnny Marks brought the soldiers back home when he played and sang 'Rudolph'. Me, I had a rough start—I was bearded then, and beards were often associated with the anti-war movement. One soldier told me that when he and his buddies first saw me they thought about "teaching me a lesson". However, my obvious concern with their situation and my being there to entertain them turned things around, and they comfortably shared their war stories with me. It was Harry Woods, though, who was a big inspiration to the wounded. They loved that Harry had overcome a deformed, fingerless left hand, and could bang out a mean ragtime bass line with it at the piano. Harry's songs might have been written in the 1920s and '30s, but they were just what the hospital doctors ordered. When I met Harry just before we left for the Far East, he was unaware that his song 'Try a Little Tenderness', written in 1932, was high on the charts once again thanks to Otis Redding's big recording of the song.

We never did get past the Philippines because the Tet Offensive got under way and the USO had to scramble to get us out of the area. Travel was a mess, but they managed to route us through Hong Kong and then Hawaii, where I stayed for a couple of days before heading home.

In 2001, disaster in the form of terrorists hijacking and flying planes into the Twin Towers of the World Trade Center struck New York City. Once again singers were called on to perform for our

Entertaining the troops in the Philippines

heroic first responders, the firemen who had lost so many of their comrades as they bravely fought to save victims of the inferno. At one such benefit I was asked to sing 'Roses Are Red'. The audience sang along, and behind me a chorus of more than two dozen of the busiest New York studio singers sang their hearts out. And although I believe that our singing for these heroes did bring them some solace, the opportunity to entertain them was very meaningful for all of us who sang for them.

THE MOST BEAUTIFUL SHIP IN THE WORLD

Thanks to my early hits I continued traveling the world whenever an opportunity to do so presented itself. In 1969 I took a gig singing on the SS *France*, the beautiful French Line flagship known as the Versailles of the Atlantic because of her rich décor. I traveled the Caribbean three times, bringing along a couple of my friends to be my conductors on those trips. Charles Randolph Grean, who wrote the #1 Phil Harris record 'The Thing' in 1950, conducted on two of the trips. Joe Rene, who arranged, produced, and co-wrote Bobby Lewis' 1961 smash #1 hit 'Tossin' and Turnin'' (under his wife's name, Malou Rene) conducted on one.

I worked mostly with young singing groups and older comedians. The cruise ships' rule seemed to be to hire the up-and-coming and the over-the-hill. I seemed to be an exception to the rule because the trapped audiences knew my repertoire of songs and loved singing along with the original artist.

I was told that passengers could order anything they wanted to eat, even elephant meat. (I didn't want to eat an elephant.) We performers didn't starve either. However, the dining room waiters did not love serving the entertainers. We ate in the children's room after the kids were done. That meant that the waiters, who must have done something wrong to be assigned to that room, had to stay late for us. They were rather brusque and, of course, they were always in a hurry. Don't forget, the ship's staff were French, and a bottle of white wine and another of red were always available when we sat down for our meals. So my fellow performers and I got even for the waiters' poor attitude by looking them right in the eye, taking a bottle of white in the one hand, a bottle of red in the other, and pouring both into one glass and creating a rosé right in front of their eyes. That act of creativity was not appreciated. If looks could kill, we would never have gotten off the ship.

The ship had a rather uncomfortable chore for male members of the staff, a gathering that we had to attend. Because of the cost of the trip, there were many, many older widows aboard. It was most likely one of the first times in a long, long time that they were off by themselves or with a group of women that shared the very same sad experience. I would guess that the cruise was an attempt to put some joy and excitement back into their lives. The women were invited to join the male staff at the gathering, which featured wine and cocktails. I can attest to the fact that many of the male attendees left the party with sore backsides that day.

Performing on ships in the 1960s and '70s was not nearly as difficult as it is for today's ship entertainers. All I had to do was perform once on a trip southbound and once more on the way home. I once sang on a 19-day trip—which meant 2 days on and

17 off. (I smiled at the memory as I wrote that last sentence.) I had plenty of time to spend on the beautiful beaches of the Caribbean with the ship's musicians who, because they worked six months on the ship and six months off, knew the best local beaches and the local people who swam there. They might not have been the world's greatest musicians, but they were very appreciative of their time on the ship, even though the job took them away from their families for half a year at a time. And of course, some of them took advantage of their time away from home.

There were, as you might guess, several shipboard romances during my trips, and I was involved in one. A young folk music quartet was hired to open the show for me, and I was immediately attracted to one of the female singers. We clicked, even though she, the rest of her group and I knew that her fiancé would be waiting at the group's last port of call. But, hell, the days were sun-filled, the evenings star-filled and we liked each other a lot. Aboard ship it was impossible to keep secrets, so quite a few of the ship's staff were aware that something was going on. They all knew that she was engaged, that soon she'd be leaving the ship and that her fiancé would be waiting on the dock to greet her. I can still recall a bunch of people leaning over the rail with me that day, watching the dreaded reunion, and everyone being extra nice to an obviously depressed me. Paul Parnes and I once wrote a song with a title that would've been appropriate for that romance: 'You'll Forget It, I'll Forget It—But I'll Remember'.

Cruise lines have changed the rules since I entertained on them. Now entertainers get on the ship at the point of embarkation, perform that evening, disembark at the next port and board another ship, perform that evening, and so on and so on until their booking is over. That's got to be one exhausting gig.

The SS *France*'s epilogue is a sad one: that beautiful ship was scrapped in 1980.

Chapter 7
AFTER ALL, IT IS CALLED THE MUSIC BUSINESS

A SHORT LESSON IN MUSIC ECONOMICS

In the late '70s, I was asked to write a song to promote the annual March of Dimes' Walk-a-Thon. I wrote it with Fred Tobias. The music department loved the song, I produced the track, and they were very happy with the results. However, it took four more years for the March of Dimes to call me back for more music. Once again, I asked Freddy to write a song with me and we came through with another successful piece for them.

I wanted to see how the music was synced with the film, so I invited myself over to the film editor's office. He was happy to have me watch him "do his thing". We got to talking and I told him that I was confused about why the March of Dimes had taken four years to call me back for another job after that first successful campaign that I produced for them. I said, "Since the organization is a charitable one, I charged them much less than I ordinarily would charge for writing and producing a musical track." He laughed. "That's the reason, brother. You were too cheap for them. Every year they submit a budget based on their expenses for the previous year, and you were just too inexpensive for their budgeting." He told me that he charged extra when he worked for them. It didn't feel right to me, but this time I charged them the same as I would charge a profit-making business for my work (I just couldn't see my way to charging the March of Dimes any more than I would charge a non-charitable organization) and I was called back and worked for them for three more years in a row.

Lesson depressingly learned.

Chapter 8
WELL HELLO, JOANNIE

BACK IN THE GAME (JOANNIE)

In 1978 I wrote a song with Fred Tobias. I sent my demo down to one of my music heroes: the legendary guitarist, and head of RCA Nashville's operations, Chet Atkins. Chet liked the song and said that he'd like to record it with me. *Be still, my heart.* Chet Atkins producing my record—that would have been my dream come true. Chet told me, however, that unbeknown to me he'd had some health issues and was no longer head of recording at RCA. He'd have to get an okay from his successor at that position, Jerry Bradley, the son of Owen Bradley, Decca Records' Nashville head of productions. That uncomfortable news became disastrous news; Jerry Bradley turned the project down. As you can imagine, I was heartbroken, but not for long.

Somewhere along the way I had met Jimmy "the Wiz" Wisner, a major force in music in his own right. He had his first success as a jazz pianist in his hometown, Philadelphia, with the Jimmy Wisner Trio. His classical music training led him to record a rock 'n' roll version of an Edvard Grieg Piano Concerto, which he titled 'Asia Minor'. He recorded the song under the name Kokomo. (He didn't use his real name because he was afraid that he'd lose his jazz audience.) 'Asia Minor' got to #8 on the *Billboard* charts in 1961. It also rose to #35 in England in spite of being banned by the BBC for violating standards that they found abusive and distortive to a classical music piece.

His early jazz background led to accompanying and conducting work with Mel Tormé, nicknamed "The Velvet Fog", singers Carmen McRae and Dakota Staton, and the Hi-Lo's. However, Jimmy was best known for his producing and arranging. A small list of the artists that he worked with reads like a Who's Who of the music world: Tony Bennett, Iggy Pop, Carly Simon, Barbra Streisand, Robert Goulet and Tommy James. (Tommy and Jimmy shared a 52-year relationship that started with Jimmy's arrangement of 'I Think We're Alone Now', a song that reached #4 on *Billboard's* Hot 100 for Tommy in 1967). Jimmy was also known internationally for his work with Brazil's Roberto Carlos and France's Sasha Distel. And as a leader in the music business, he was the head of A & R at Columbia Records in New York under Clive Davis, and a governor on the Board of the Recording Academy, the group that awards the Grammys.

When Jimmy and I first met, I played him the song that Jerry Bradley had refused to allow Chet Atkins to record with me. Jimmy

Jimmy Wisner and me in London for the *Top of the Pops*

loved it and we flew off to Nashville to record it. We contracted one of Nashville's most popular studio singers, Lea Jane Berinati, to sing the chorus:

> Hello, this is Joannie
> I'm sorry that I'm not home
> But if you leave me your name and number
> I promise soon as I get in I'll phone

The song was 'Hello, This Is Joannie (The Telephone Answering Machine Song)' and it was to put me back on the national and international record charts after almost a 20-year hiatus.

Jimmy and I walked the recording over to Spring Records, owned by the Rifkind brothers, Roy and Julie. Spring was well known for soul music artists like Millie Jackson and Joe Simon. So why me and why 'Hello, This Is Joannie', a pop-country song recorded in Nashville? For whatever reason, the brothers signed the song and it took off. It was #1 on many of America's big city, country charts but could only make its way to the #57 spot on *Billboard's* national Hot 100 Country charts. Internationally it was bigger than it was here at home. It climbed the Australian charts to #2 and reached the #6 spot in England.

In January 1979, Jimmy and I flew to London where I was to appear on *Top of The Pops*, England's number one pop show. We met with Roger Easterby, Polydor Records' promotion man. (Spring's records were issued on the Polydor label in the UK with a label credit.) Jimmy, Roger and I all agreed that the appearance would put 'Joannie' on the road to #1. The next day I had a long interview with journalists from popular teen magazines and a photo session at Jack Barclay's Rolls Royce showroom in Berkley Square. Roger put seven attractive young women who worked at the showroom in the back seat of a Rolls Royce convertible and sat me in the front to remind people about 'Seven Little Girls Sitting in the Back Seat', some 20 years before 'Hello, This Is Joannie' hit the charts. I went to bed that evening exhausted, but looking forward to the next day's show.

I had already discovered that Roger was a master jokester, so when he burst into my hotel room and said, "Sorry, Paul, but you won't be appearing on the show today," I was sure that he was pulling my leg. He had to tell me three times before I realized that he wasn't kidding. He explained that the *Top of the Pops*' rules stated that a song had to be in the Top 10 and moving up the charts before the artist could appear on the show. We were all sure that 'Joannie' would meet those goals. However, it turned out that quietly, Chrysalis Records hadn't reported sales of Blondie's 'Heart of Glass' for a week and then reported the record's two weeks sales total, which was very high. Those figures landed 'Heart of Glass' in the #5 spot on the charts and kept 'Joannie' from moving up.

Top of the Pops said that if they could get a copy of my 'Seven Little Girls' appearance on *The Dick Clark Show* by the time they were due to go on the air, they would allow me to perform. They tried to get a copy from Dick's production company, but it was all in vain. There was no way that they could get it in time and the focus of Jimmy's and my trip was snatched away from us at the last minute. Roger did the best he could to have me make the most of my trip. He had me flown up to Scotland to promote 'Joannie'. The record company's local promotion man drove me on a whirlwind tour of radio stations from Glasgow to Edinburgh. Put a young promotion man into an automobile on an icy road on a freezing cold day and he will get you where you're going—no matter what. I'll never forget that drive. Nor will I forget the haggis and the neeps & tatties that I felt honor-bound to try while I was in Scotland.

Roger Easterby has got to be the world's best record promotion man—ever. He took me to see the Osmonds' performance at the Royal Albert Hall and there he performed a feat of promotional magic. He told me that he'd like to introduce me to Donny Osmond and led me to a dining area where Donny was enjoying just sitting alone and eating his dinner. Roger introduced us, and mentioned my record 'Hello, This is Joannie' and some of my other successes. Donny stood up and came around the table to shake my hand and Roger snapped a photo. That photo later came out in the music magazine *Cash Box* over the headline, "Paul Evans takes time out of his busy schedule to say hello to Donny Osmond." Roger had done it again! He and I had so much fun together that we bonded and have been great friends ever since.

I had heard that 'Hello, This Is Joannie' was doing well in South Africa. So when one of my wife's friends who had moved to South

'Hello, This Is Joannie' publicity photo

Africa to be with her boyfriend—a park ranger—said that she could help us put together a photo safari in the bush, Susan and I jumped at the offer.

Our first stop was Johannesburg, where I called the South African publisher of 'Joannie', Kevin O'Hara. When I introduced myself, he exploded, "Wow! Your timing is great. 'Hello, This Is Joannie' is #1 here!" The kicker, unfortunately, was that it was #1 on the *white* South African charts. Okay, #1 on the white charts in South Africa should probably bring in some small amount of writing royalties, but Kevin explained it wouldn't even do that. His boss was a notoriously bad payer. However, Kevin was a terrific guy, so he treated Susan and me to a couple of lunches and dinners while we were in town—in lieu of the royalties I wouldn't receive.

As part of our photo safari, we traveled to a remote camp in Botswana, across the Chobe River from Namibia, where we had to be sprayed with an anti-tsetse fly repellent before entering the camp's clearing. We really were in the middle of nowhere. When

Roger Easterby, the world's best promotion man—ever

all the guests gathered around a campfire that night, the woman who ran the camp asked me what I did at home. I explained that I was a singer. "Do you have a record out that we might know?" she asked. I told her that I doubted that she and her guests would know 'Hello, This Is Joannie'. And with that, everyone began to sing my song—in a tented camp surrounded by tsetse flies and the sounds of lions roaring, somewhere in Botswana. *That* was a special moment!

Another day, Susan and I ate lunch in a restaurant in a boma, a community or livestock enclosure, surrounded by a fence. However, at a safari lodge, it might be a place to enjoy meals or to be entertained. My record of 'Joannie' caught the restaurant manager's attention, and he asked one of his staff to perform for us. The shy musician entertained us with a traditional African melody on his traditional African mouth bow, which uses the mouth as a resonator. Just another special moment brought to Susan and me, courtesy of 'Hello, this is Joannie'.

CAUGHT IN A TRAP (WISNER)

To soothe the loss of the *Top of the Pops*' appearance, Jimmy and I upgraded our homeward-bound plane tickets to British Airway's Concorde. This might have not been a good way for Jimmy to relax because he was a big man and Concorde was a small plane. But it did get us back to home and to a meeting with Spring Records very quickly.

We expected champagne and caviar to celebrate our trip. Unfortunately, it turned out that the only ones not pleased with how well 'Hello, This Is Joannie' had done were Roy and Julie Rifkind, Spring's owners. When Jimmy and I walked into their office, instead of congratulating us, they greeted us with stony faces and announced that they had decided that the next Paul Evans release would be a Rhythm and Blues record. Impossible! I thought that Jimmy was going to leap across the table that separated the brothers from us.

I guess that, even though they understood how to promote R & B records, they were out of their league when it came to country or country-pop records that Jimmy and I were apparently good at making. Ed Salamon, who programmed New York City's big country radio station, WHN, told me that 'Joannie' had hit #1 on his station despite the fact that Spring Records never contacted him. Then we discovered that Spring Records had not promoted our records to any country music station around the country.

When we refused to accept their condition for another recording session, Roy and Julie told us that they were releasing us from our contract. We left the office confused and angry, but thinking that Spring Records had created an unusual opportunity for us. We were coming off a successful record and we would form our own record company. Sounds good, doesn't it? It wasn't.

Jimmy and I fell into a trap, a no-no in the record business. We moved too fast. We recorded a single, 'One Night Led To Two', which I co-wrote with Bob Alan, and backed it with 'Hangin' Out and Hangin' In', co-written with Paul Parnes. We also hired a small Nashville distributor to distribute our new label, Cinnamon Records, but our label quickly ran out of money and the record was a disappointment. So Jimmy and I admitted our mistake and dissolved Cinnamon.

Spring Records did release two more Paul Evans singles after 'Joannie' before our trip to England. However, Spring refused to release an album that Jimmy and I had recorded. That album, *Hello, This is Paul Evans,* was released in England on Polydor Records.

One of those two singles that Spring released was a real heartbreaker for me. After my divorce, my ex moved away with our daughter in tow. Every Sunday I would drive up to see my young daughter and we would wind up at a kid's film, eating at McDonald's, or going to a park. All the things that divorced daddies do. One afternoon, I drove her back to her house and as I turned to give her a kiss goodbye and assure her that I'd be back the next Sunday, she noticed her uncle's car in the driveway. "Oh, goodie. Uncle Jackie's here," she said and jumped out of the car. And there I was, sitting alone. No hug, no kiss goodbye. No chance to say anything.

My co-writer, Paul Parnes pressed me to recreate the emotions that I felt at that moment in the car. I did, and we wrote 'Disneyland Daddy'. Here's the chorus of the song:

I'm a Disneyland Daddy
Bet you think I'm a big, old dancin' bear
Ronald McDonald, Sesame Street
And a puppy dog all in one
I'm a Disneyland Daddy
But you're home with your mommy when the day is done
And I take off the mask that I've been wearin'
Soon as you kiss me goodbye
And I turn away to hide the teardrops
In your Disneyland Daddy's eye

This was a song that I had written from deep emotions, and which I truly wanted to share with an audience. I actually cried in pain during the recording session. Jimmy and I later discovered that many radio programmers were divorced and in a similar situation as the song's theme. We were told that it caused them pain and they just couldn't get themselves to program it. But in spite of the lack of record company support and programmer resistance, 'Disneyland Daddy' did manage to follow 'Hello, This is Joannie' onto the *Billboard* Country charts, getting to the #81 spot in 1979. And Cinnamon Records' only release, my recording of 'One Night Led to Two', followed up at #80 in 1980. Considering my New York accent, country music has been very good to me.

Chapter 9
SCRATCHING THAT ITCH

IF YOU HAVE AN ITCH, SCRATCH IT (ROCKABILLY HILL)

In 1978, before 'Joannie' was released, I got an itch to perform in front of audiences in and around New York City. So I put a band together and called it Rockabilly Hill. The basic band consisted of bassist Frank Baier, who I met while singing on jingles in studios; Jerry Holland on guitar, who introduced me to Fred Caruso at the piano; and Jimmy Young, a New York studio session's star on drums. Jerry, I should add, was (and remains) my nephew, who was just getting started professionally. In 1996 he would write 'Friends', a country hit for John Michael Montgomery, and presently he writes songs for and works clubs with his jazz-singing wife, Sony.

The band rehearsed at Chappell Music's small recording studio, where we laid down some rockabilly songs on a disc. I used the disc to show what we sounded like to club managers when mentioning my hits just didn't do it for us. Our toughest gig was in 1978, when we played in a musician's hangout, Possible 20, on West 55th Street in New York City. When I arrived at the club that evening, I discovered that their air conditioning wasn't working. New York was in the middle of a heat wave, it was over 90° outside and who knows how hot inside, especially on the stage, but we had an audience, and the band and some special guests were willing to sweat it out. We were all pros and decided that the show would go on.

Very recently Susan and I came across a video of the performance. I must admit that I'd forgotten how much fun rockabilly songs were to perform in front of an audience, and how much I miss performing live. The band performed my Kalin Twins' hit song 'When'; my own hit recording of 'Midnight Special'; and rockabilly standards like Eddie Cochran's 'Summertime Blues', Don Gibson's 'Oh, Lonesome Me' and Guy Mitchell's 'Singin' the Blues', with Jerry and Frank adding some harmonies for me. But the highlight of the evening was when I invited my special guests, four women that I had befriended in the New York studios, onto the stage. It was a treat for me to sing 'Seven Little Girls Sitting in the Back Seat' and 'Roses Are Red (My Love)' with the beautiful voices of Arlene Martell, Jeannie Thomas, Terry Textor and Judy Saul harmonizing with me. And professionals all, they stuck around for our second set in what must have been 100° heat on the stage.

After Jimmy and I returned from our trip to England and 'Hello, This is Joannie' landed in the #1 spot on New York's country station, WHN, I revamped Rockabilly Hill and returned to playing clubs and school auditoriums in the area. But when 'Joannie' lost its spot on the charts, it lost its drawing power and the band sadly broke up, never to return again.

OH WHAT A BEAUTIFUL MORNING (CBS AND SPORTS)

In 1987 CBS-TV cancelled its morning show, appropriately named *The Morning Program*. It was to be replaced with a new show with a new format, *CBS This Morning*. The director of the show was to be Duke Struck, the former director of the *Robert MacNeil Report* on Public TV and *Good Morning America* on ABC, and the future director of *The Oprah Winfrey Show*. Duke knew me and asked me to take a shot at writing a new theme for the new show. Of course I said, "Yes."

I decided to write the music with Red Nienkirchen, a talented writer and arranger. CBS provided us with a budget big enough to produce an on-air- quality recording. This was presented at a major meeting of CBS executives, including Duke and the producer of the show. The producer wanted to use the *CBS Evening News* theme because *CBS This Morning* was to feature "harder" news than the competing networks' morning shows. However, Duke wanted a unique theme for the show. He prevailed, and Red's and my theme was chosen.

I remember the date of the meeting because it was the Wednesday before Thanksgiving and the show was debuting on the following Monday. Red and I would have to put together lots of different versions of the theme—full versions, intros, outros, piano solos, specifically timed versions (:03, :05, :08 seconds, etc.), for lead-ins and -outs of commercials and guest interviews—by Saturday. Thanksgiving would be just another workday for us. While Red would write the arrangements, I would collect musicians, instruments and a studio for a Friday session. Television is a visual business. Music is often a last-minute thought, and obviously our theme was no exception to the rule. Red and I got everything done and had the final music messengered over to CBS. Now for some sleep.

Turned out, that wasn't in the script.

On Saturday morning, my phone rang. It was Duke and the producer. They needed some changes and additions, and the show was just two days off. That meant that we'd have to go back into the studio on the Sunday of the four-day Thanksgiving holiday. I very naively asked if they could use what we had already delivered to them on Monday's show, and let us put what they needed together after the weekend for their Tuesday show. The suggestion was greeted by silence on the other side of the phone. Red and I would just have to make the changes that they needed for their Monday opening.

That meant having the studio opened for us on Sunday morning. Luckily, Red and I knew the studio manager and, bless him, he promised to come in from home to accommodate us. Then there was the matter of finding musicians who hadn't gone out of town for the holiday. Again we lucked out and many of our first-call musicians were able to do the job for us. We worked all day Sunday into the early hours of Monday, when Red and I finally finished recording and mixing the tracks. Susan had accompanied me to the studio that Sunday, so she and I took the tape from the studio directly over to CBS's West Side studio. The show's offices weren't open yet, but we managed to talk our way into the empty waiting room. There we sat, studio tape clutched tightly in my hands. The show's staff started showing up, but we wouldn't give the tape to anyone but Duke. When he got there, we gave him the tape, he thanked us, and we went home to try to get a couple of hours of sleep.

A restful sleep was impossible, however. Although CBS had spent a lot of money on our theme, we had never been given official assurance that the theme would be ours. We set our alarm clock to just before 7:00 a.m., when *CBS This Morning* would air. When the alarm woke us, we turned the TV on and heard the show's theme. It was Red's and my music. So we turned off the TV and went back to sleep, happy with the results of those four days of musical trials and tribulations.

Our theme was used for a little over three years. Then one morning I turned on the *CBS This Morning* show and heard Rogers and Hammerstein's 'Oh, What a Beautiful Morning', from their Broadway musical *Oklahoma!,* used as an interim opening theme. Red and I were given no warning that the show was dropping our original theme and that we wouldn't be invited to compete for the new one. The show had a new director. Duke Struck had been our man, and now some other writers had found their own man. Game over.

Duke Struck was also responsible for another area of the music world where I eventually had success: Sports Music. He liked my work on the morning show and started to call me when he was the Coordinating Director of Live Sports at CBS and needed music for a show. One day I was at home when Duke called and asked me if I could create a piano version of 'Raindrops Are Falling on My Head' for one of his shows. "By the way, I need it in time to have it on the air in two hours." Of course I completed the assignment on time. You had to be prepared to put everything else aside and accommodate the producers and just understand that that's the way it worked in TV land.

I was writing with a young talented songwriter, Paul Rolnick, and I brought him into the field of Sports Music with me. The music required a specific structure. For the most part it had to be aggressive music and yet not get in the way of the sportscaster. Believe it or not, there was football music, basketball music, baseball music and so on. There was background music and there was theme music. Theme music was the prize. It paid much better per performance than background music did. Paul and I won our share of competitions, and since he was a wiz at computer music and quickly learned the dos and don'ts of the sports music field, we could work at my computer in the comfort of my home office. When Duke left CBS to work as an independent director, his assistant Susan Reisinger continued to call on Paul and me when she needed music.

IF AT FIRST YOU DON'T SUCCEED (WELL, YOU KNOW)

After our Cinnamon Records debacle, the team of Wisner and Evans might have learned their lesson, but I was determined to dream on. So I packed my bags in 1993 and ran back to Nashville to cut four more songs.

Nashville was a great music town, and within the music business, a bit friendlier than the New York music scene. Every time I travelled to Nashville, I was amazed at how other writers would let me know which artists were looking for songs. Yes, in New York we all knew when Elvis was coming up for a session, but those writers who had any knowledge about which other artists might be looking for material held that information close to the chest. Coming down from New York, I had to learn some of the customs of the city. On my first trip to Nashville to show my songs, I was alone and rather lonely. When I left someone's office, they would generally say, "Now y'all come back and see us, hear?" and I would answer, "Wow. That would be great." But instead of an invitation, all I received was an embarrassing silence. I was confused. Why ask me to come back to see them but not set a date? So when Bob Tubert, a Nashville writer, asked me to "Come back and see us, hear?", I described my dilemma. He laughed and explained that it was just a nice Southern way to end a meeting, something like a New Yorker's "Have a great day." But Bob did more than explain, he invited me over for a barbecue at his home that evening. I had made my first Nashville friend.

Here are the three songs that I recorded:

'Willie's Sung with Everyone (But Me)'

> *My daughter once complained to me that Willie Nelson had sung with everyone but her father. (On the record, I mention 84 duets that Willie had recorded.) So I wrote a song about a man who has a dream that he sings a song with Ol' Willie on TV and becomes a star as a result. When he wakes up, he tries to turn the dream into a reality. Finding Willie in a barroom one day, he sings a Willie*

Nelson song but gets the words all wrong. Willie leaves, and the dreamer realizes that his "career was over before it begun." (I claim writers' privilege to the word "begun". It rhymed.) I tried every which way to get the song to Willie. I called his fan club president, who brushed me off. When I performed on an Oldies Show, I ran into Don Cherry, who told me that he played golf with Willie and would give him a copy of the record. I called Willie's manager's office and I found out the name of a publicity office that did some work for him. Alas, it wasn't meant to be. I never did find out if Willie ever got to hear my tribute to him. However, I was elated when I found out that Sony Music Special Products had released a CD, Willie Nelson – 22 Legendary Duets, which included a bonus song: my recording of 'Willie's Sung With Everyone (But Me)'.

'Santa's Stuck up in the Chimney'

Santa gets stuck in a chimney and everyone must push, tug, pull and shove—to the sounds of Santa moaning and groaning—because "there'll be no Christmas till they set him free."

'The Beautiful Grass of Kentucky'

More Folk than Country, with a sensational lyric by Al Byron about Ol' Caleb Carew; a mean-tempered planter who married an orphaned young woman and "took her to bed." But the beautiful grass of Kentucky turns blue and in sympathy, nature ruins everything that Caleb owns.

I hired some of those fabled "Nashville musicians" (whose names time has stolen from me) and three great studio singers; Lea Jane Berinati, Danny Bailey, and Jeff Pearles. Then I hustled back to New York to record a fourth song with some wonderful jazz musicians and background vocals by Group 5ive:

'The Yodelin' Jazzman'

My song about a young singer who tries to sing jazz, but every time he tries to scat (innovate vocally) he winds up yodeling. However, he does get a call from the Blue Note jazz club in New York, but unfortunately for his jazz career, he breaks into a yodel again.

I was so happy with the results of the recording sessions and certain that there was a hit record among those four sides that I jumped in with both feet.

I decided to form my own label (sound familiar?), Garden of Eden Records, and release an EP with all four songs on it. I titled the EP "Willie's Sung with Everyone (But Me)" and hired an artist to create the cover art—a sketch of Willie and me standing around a microphone with an X over the two of us. After all, Willie had sung with everyone—but me. The artist also designed a logo for the label. I hired Nashville's Shepherd Marketing to distribute the EP and promote the title track. (Still no inner voice suggesting that I slow down and take stock of the situation.) Then Susan and I started stuffing envelopes with the EP and mailing them to a list of country music radio supervisors and DJs around the country.

The result was not what I had been so absolutely sure that it would be. In fact, there was hardly any response. Just to rub it in, when I brought the record up to the newest country station in New York, the FM station WYNY radio (WHN radio had changed to sports radio WFAN in 1987), the programmer, a former rock 'n' roll DJ, told me that he couldn't play any record by or about Willie Nelson because the station's new policy was not to play records by country artists that came before Clint Black in 1989. When I asked him (sarcastically, I admit): "What will you do if Willie has another hit record?", he gave me the stink eye and said that he'd cross that bridge when he came to it.

So what did I do? I listened to that nasty little devil sitting on my shoulder and decided to immediately abandon working on 'Willie' and quickly put out a single of 'Santa's Stuck Up in the Chimney'. Uh-oh. Here I was, breaking a rule again: "Think before you jump into any new enterprise, especially if it's not based on solid information." Too many things can go wrong and leave you pounding your head and wondering, "What in the world was I thinking?" But I obviously wasn't into thinking at the time and anyway, what could go wrong? Christmas was on the horizon and it was a perfect time to release 'Santa'. I asked a cartoonist friend of mine, Bob Schochet, to create cover art for the single and had Harry Hirsch's always-reliable Digi Rom master the record.

Okay, here's what could go wrong: the first sample of the test single had a major error built into it—a skip on it that was very obvious—and by the time I received the corrected sample it was too close to Christmas to manufacture, release and promote the record. I was stuck. I had neither the know-how nor the experience to cope with the situation that I found myself in. I'd fallen into the same trap that Jimmy Wisner and I had fallen into with Cinnamon Records. I had to admit that Garden of Eden Records wasn't well thought out at all and I dissolved it before I could do any more damage. Was this a lesson finally learned? Well, I've been thinking lately of producing a CD with some of the demos I've created over the years. Someone, please stop me!

Several years later, in 2007, I decided to go in a different direction with 'Santa'. I found a Disney animator, Llyn Hunter, whose work I liked, and I asked her to create a YouTube video for the song. She did a great job and this time I got the video up at the beginning of October, in plenty of time for Christmas.

Actually, the video has been a success for me. As of now, the video has gathered well over 3,000,000 views on YouTube, and has become a favorite at many primary schools' Christmas shows. And, oh yes, the money I earned from performances on YouTube has been enough to recoup the money that I spent on the video. 'Santa's Stuck up in the Chimney' is another good reason for me to love the holiday season.

Chapter 10
THE WORLD IS MY OYSTER—SOMETIMES YOU JUST HAVE TO PRY IT OPEN

ALL THAT JAZZ

I always considered myself a "B" team member of the New York City jingle world's cadre of singers. I loved singing and I loved that jingle producers thought enough of my voice and my musicality to hire me for solo and for group work. I always thought that I could've joined the "A" team if I hadn't run down to Nashville anytime a record session was available for me. There was a large group of quality singers waiting to break into the jingles field and if you missed a couple of sessions for a producer, they'd find someone else to take your spot and you'd have to fight your way back into their first team.

In the New York studios I sang jingles alongside of some very talented singers, and five of them had formed a jazz group, Group 5ive. They had a great reputation doing gigs around town and had sung in an Atlantic City casino. However, they'd just lost their baritone. The four remaining members asked me to join their group. They were Lenny Roberts, a fine musician and singer as well as a terrific writer, and three of the best female singers in New York City. Helen Miles had sung on Broadway as an understudy for Ethel Merman, appeared in regional theaters and was often called on to put a singing group together for a producer. She always sang the

Lenny, Arlene, Annette, Helen, and me

alto part in the group. Arlene Martell, the "Queen of Jingles". and Annette Sanders, a great club performer as well as a first call on many jingle sessions, had similar ranges but a different vocal timbre (the quality of their sound), so they switched the lead depending on the style of the song.

Paul Evans, Jazzer? Well, I had sung rock 'n' roll, country-pop, and had plenty of experience singing in groups thanks to jingles and backing up soloists on record dates. Also, I was a good sight-reader, so why not accept their confidence in me and give it a shot?

I didn't realize just how important the ability to sight-read would be. The group had worked with different arrangers, but their main go-to was Michael Abene, a brilliant arranger noted for his complex charts. One popular and great jazz guitarist often worked for Michael. At one recording session, Mike was handing out music charts for the musicians and when the guitarist took a look at the chart he was given, he reportedly threw it on the floor, stepped on it, and said, "This time, Abene, you've gone too far."

Of course. we not only had to read the charts, we'd be singing in front of audiences, so we would have to memorize them. Thank goodness for the computer and music apps. To memorize my part, I'd write it into one side of a stereo track and write the other four parts into the other side. Then I'd play the parts back, each time slowly lowering the volume of my part while singing along with it, until all that was left for me to sing along with were the other four parts. As the songs grew more challenging, I would mutter to myself, "This time, Abene, you've gone too far."

Rehearsals were pretty intense. But I soon caught up to everyone and we prepared for my first gig with the group at the Chez Odette in New Hope, Pennsylvania. (The restaurant was where Jessica Savage, one of the first women to anchor an evening network newscast, had dined before riding in a car that crashed over a barrier into the Delaware Canal, where she drowned. The incident made nationwide news.) During soundchecking at the restaurant, some very tough-looking, big men took seats in the back of the room and stared at us. Since this was my first gig with the group, I was nervous and sure that they were there to throw me into the canal if I screwed up. But I didn't and so they didn't. Then the room filled with customers. We sang to an appreciative audience and Paul Evans was officially a part of Group 5ive.

What a great and different experience for me. We sang to sold-out audiences in area clubs in New York City, New Jersey and Pennsylvania, and as far away as Battle Creek, Michigan. We sang in college auditoriums and in concert halls. Audiences, young and old, appreciated how effortlessly we performed our complicated arrangements of the standards that we sang for them. Yet one of our best moments at every performance was when we sang our 'Jingle Medley, a medley of jingles that each of us had sung on. They reacted with applause for each song in the medley as though it was an old friend that they were happy to hear from again.

At one concert in New York we sang, a cappella, 'Two For the Road' written by Henry Mancini. We didn't know it, but Hank was in our audience, and when we finished his song, he leapt to his feet and led a standing ovation for us. Backstage, he congratulated us for "singing the song without a net". He was referring to our singing a very difficult a cappella arrangement and staying on pitch from top to bottom without relying on an instrument. Other well-known singers came backstage after our performance to congratulate us for our performance. It was very heady stuff.

In 1997 we booked a week in Philadelphia with Peter Nero and the Philadelphia Pops Orchestra at the Academy of Music, the oldest opera house in the United States still used for concerts. When we first got to the Academy for a rehearsal and I looked out at the auditorium from the stage, my jaw dropped. It was breathtakingly beautiful. Built between 1855 and 1857, it was decorated in crimson and gold, and had a 16-foot (4.8-m) chandelier hanging from the high ceiling. When we began to rehearse, I realized how much care the builders had taken with the acoustic properties of the hall. Sensational! And having that large orchestra behind Group 5ive pushed us to give some of our best performances ever. As we left the stage, the orchestra members gave us a standing ovation—a rare event.

But probably the biggest and highest point of our group's career was being asked to sing at Jazz Festivals in Europe, where jazz is bigger than it is here at home. The tour lasted from July 10 until July 26, 1991. We sang in Denmark at the North Sea Jazz Festival in The Hague and at the Kridthuset Club in Copenhagen. Our next stop was a major festival in Arhus, Denmark. After Arhus, we had to take a couple of days off from our European tour to honor a commitment to appear at New York City's 92nd Street YMHA. We had tried to get out of the commitment by offering Dick Hyman, who ran the show, a well-known group to replace us if he would just reschedule our appearance. But Dick was not sympathetic to our situation at all. He wanted Group 5ive. I asked the group to allow me to fake getting sick, but they wouldn't go for it. So we had to fly back from Denmark to New York, and then, a day later, back to Pori, Finland for the Pori Jazz festival. We finished our tour in Helsingborg, Sweden—exhausted.

At one of our performances, we were given a spot following the Manhattan Transfer onto the stage. This was, of course, terrible scheduling. The Transfer and Group 5ive sang similar songs and harmonies. We were five people, they were four—that was our only advantage. They were much better known than we were and most people in the audience of 9,000 had come especially to watch them.

As we came on stage, we noticed that people were beginning to leave. However, once we started singing, they turned around and came back and showed their appreciation for us by staying until we sang our last song. What a great moment for our group.

At another outdoor concert in Europe, Helen was singing her solo song, 'I Dreamed a Dream' from *Les Miserables*, when the lights and our microphones suddenly went off. Helen, the pro that she was, asked the crowd to hush and she went on to sing the song a cappella. It was a very stirring performance, and the audience went crazy for her. It drew sustained applause and gave me an idea. I gathered the group that evening and suggested that we have the electrician pull the plug at every one of Helen's solo performances in the future. The group shot the idea down. They didn't like the "dishonesty of the move". Yes, it would have been dishonest, but audiences would have loved it. I knew it would work because I'd seen Tommy Steele (once known as England's answer to Elvis Presley) on Broadway in *Half a Sixpence.* In one scene a dancer dropped his hat. As they continued to dance, Tommy came around, picked up the hat, flipped it to the dancer who had lost it, and never lost a step. The audience, including my wife and I, cheered and applauded. I was impressed until I talked to friends who had seen the show on different nights. They all recalled the same "spontaneous" on-stage incident.

MAGIC MOMENTS

Another great gig for the group was Public Television's *Magic Moments: The Best of '50s Pop* in 2003. We were asked to back up performers who had hits in the 1950s. It was a tough job because we were asked to sound as close as we could to the choruses that backed up the soloists on the original records.

Lenny Roberts had left the group and his replacement, Paul Rolnick, had a previous gig and couldn't join us for the show. So we called on one of the best musicians I'd ever met, Michael Mark, who wrote the theme song for the TV show *Entertainment Tonight.* Michael put the arrangements together for us and they were just great. He also sang with us. We had chosen our arranger/singer well.

But then, just to make our lives miserable and only two weeks before the show, we were told that we'd be working without music stands. We'd have to memorize our parts. And once we got to the Taj Mahal in Atlantic City, New Jersey and began rehearsals, we discovered that because many of the groups were aging, they had to sing their hits in a lower key than the original recordings. We'd been told that we would be singing in the original and now had to adjust our notes to accommodate the changes. *Magic Moments* was a tough gig. In fact, Helen Miles, who had sung in almost every area of entertainment that you could sing in, said that it was the toughest job she'd ever had the pleasure of taking part in.

Yes, it was a difficult assignment, but it was also lots of fun. I was singing with some of the artists that I'd grown up listening to. We backed up the following artists:

Patti Page	'How Much Is That Doggie In The Window?' and 'The Tennessee Waltz'.
The Four Aces	'Three Coins In The Fountain' and 'Love Is a Many Splendid Thing'.
The Four Lads	'Standing On The Corner' and 'No, Not Much'.
Mel Carter	'I'm Gonna Sit Right Down And Write Myself a Letter' and a medley of 'All Of a Sudden My Heart Sings', 'You, You, You' and 'Hold Me, Thrill Me, Kiss Me'. Mel had a bad fever, and yet he sang as though his temperature was 98.6°.
Don Cherry	'Band Of Gold'.
Lynn Evans	'Lollipop'. Health issues among the other members meant that Lynn was the only Chordette to appear on the show.
The Crew-Cuts	One of the Crew-Cuts was in the hospital, so I was asked to sing his part on 'Earth Angel'. I would be a Crew-Cut for a day—and I was excited to be one.

But it wasn't easy to be a Crew-Cut. The show's producer, TJ Lubinsky, decided that I shouldn't stand with the three remaining members of the group. He told me to sing from behind the curtain. I explained to TJ that I had to be able to watch the mouth movements of the three men in order to stay in sync with them. So he moved me in front of the curtain—but far across the stage from the Crew-Cuts. Before they sang, the group mentioned that one of their members, Rudi Maugeri, was in the hospital in very serious condition. The audience must have wondered who that strange man standing on the other side of the stage, staring at and singing with the group was. However, the cameraman, not knowing that I was to be heard and not seen, focused on me at one point, and generously, the group acknowledged my part in their performance by pointing to me while they were accepting the audience's applause.

Lubinsky had originally asked the McGuire Sisters if they wanted Group 5ive to back them up on the show. The sisters turned the offer down, but when they heard us rehearsing around the piano with Don Cherry, they changed their minds and asked if we could sing on some of their songs. We'd have been happy to accommodate them but there wasn't enough time to learn the parts. The McGuire Sisters' request had acknowledged us—we were good!

TJ told us not to bother the singers. Really? Not to bother the singers? Who were *we*? Chopped liver? When I saw Pat Boone, who was co-hosting the show, I walked over to say hello. TJ saw me headed for Pat and started to remind me "not to bother the singers". But before he could, I introduced myself to Pat as the writer of 'Johnny Will', a song of mine that Pat had recorded and took to #35 on the Hot 100 in 1961. When Pat started singing the song, TJ slunk away.

Our group also sang for an AFTRA luncheon for its broadcast journalists. As part of our performance, they had me sing my song 'Roses Are Red'. When we finished, we were walking off the stage through the audience when someone stopped me to say, "You did a great job, kid." It was Walter Cronkite, the anchorman for the *CBS Evening News* for 19 years (1962–1981) and named as "the most trusted man in America". His compliment made my day! And at an appearance set up for me by the president of the Dutch Treat Club, I played guitar and sang 'Roses' and spotted Isaac Asimov, the great science fiction writer in the audience, singing along to my song. That was another proud moment for me.

Being in Group 5ive with such well-respected singers had some other unexpected benefits for me. Helen Miles was often asked to put singing groups together for special events. Because of her, I sang on some film tracks, including two of Woody Allen's films. I was part of a Greek Chorus in his *Mighty Aphrodite*, and as a member of the Helen Miles Singers I sang "'Hooray for Captain Spaulding'" in *Everyone Says I Love You*. Groucho Marx originally performed the song in his zany film *Animal Crackers*. The chorus had to sing it in French no less, with a French tutor standing by, giving us pronunciation lessons.

But I did more than sing on *Everyone Says I Love You*. Allen's film featured actors not generally known for their singing talents, so Dick Hyman, who arranged the music for the film, had Helen Miles, Arlene Martell and myself sing the songs as a guide for the stars while he recorded the tracks. Dick was known as a very able but very tough musician, so when I hit a couple of clams while we were recording and he turned to me in front of the whole orchestra, I paled. But all he said was: "Don't worry about it, Paul. You're doing great." Whew!

Paul Rolnick, my friend and partner, and the last tenor into Group 5ive before we disbanded, contracted singing groups for some TV Soaps. He hired me when he could and we wound up on a couple of episodes of *As the World Turns* as singing police officers and singing waiters. I also sang live on the *CBS's Late Show with David Letterman*. My friend Lea Jane Berinati asked me to sing background with her when she came up from Nashville to back up her fellow Nashvillian and country music star Janie Fricke on the show. And last, but not least, I put a trio together with my friends and one-time Group 5ive members, Jeff Lyons and Paul Rolnick, to back up the rocker Robert Gordon on *Late Night with Conan O'Brien*. I remember that Conan whispered to us, "If only I could sing like you"—and the way he said it let us know that he meant it. Live TV performances were always exciting and fun, especially when friends would call and ask if it was you that they had seen on the show.

CLOVERLEAF CRISIS

Fred Tobias and I walked into a publisher's office in the Brill Building one day in the late '80s. The publisher asked us if we'd be interested in writing lyrics and music for a show written by two of his friends. Brick Hartney and Jim Arntz had written a show, book, words and music, which showed off Brick's comedic talent.

The publisher liked the show, titled *Cloverleaf Crisis*, about a beauty parlor owner who is accused of contaminating her trailer park in the outskirts of Houston, Texas with hair dyes. It was a farce with three actors, including Brick, playing multiple roles. However, no one liked the songs that the two had written. So Fred and I were called in to "save the show".

Fred had written for Broadway before: the lyrics for *Elmer Gantry* (music by Stan Lebowsky), and the song 'Take Off With Us', which was performed in the musical *All That Jazz* (again, with Lebowsky's music). I was the newbie, and when I ran into Cy Coleman, the great Broadway writer (his office was in the same building as mine), I told him that I was writing a stage show and he'd better get ready for some competition. Cy smiled, and asked, "How do you like the process, Paul?" Uh-oh. That sounded menacing. Okay. I'd been warned and I started noticing "stuff".

I knew, going into the project, that our score was replacing Brick and Jim's score, which I'm sure they had worked hard on and thought was fine. So it was only natural that some resentment would be stirred up on occasion. For instance, every once in a while they would tell us that a song that they'd originally written would fit perfectly in a specific situation in the show. We'd listen to their music—and we just never thought that it worked.

And then there was the constant battle over who had the right to write the "asides", the secrets that were whispered by the actors to the audience. Was it the book writer or the lyricist? There wasn't even a thought given to which aside worked better—just an argument over who would write it. I tried to stay neutral, but Fred was the only one with Broadway experience, and I thought that his instincts were usually better.

Brick and Jim had asked a director they knew to help us out. He was directing a musical in Pittsburgh, Pennsylvania. So we all flew down to see him "do his stuff" at a rehearsal. While he was blocking (working out a scene), he just grabbed and pushed and shoved actors around until he was happy with where he placed them. I wasn't particularly enamored with the way he handled people.

Fred and I worked our musical hearts off for *Cloverleaf Crisis*. We wrote 18 songs that were used in the show and a few more that were discarded. Writing a musical, I discovered, was a real art. The lyrics have got to keep the flow of the show moving and the music has to fit the mood of the moment. Sometimes the songs have to replace what was, without a song, an awkward spot for dialogue in the story. This was obviously going to be a low-budget show, so I made all the demos for our songs at my home office. I played the piano, used my synthesizer to fill up the band, played acoustic guitar and built up a chorus by recording several tracks myself and by occasionally having a couple of singers gather around a microphone. I didn't have any way to keep my New York City apartment as quiet as a recording studio for vocals, so we'd have to stop recording once in a while until the car horns stopped beeping or the neighbors stopped fighting or playing a competing electric guitar. (Once, when my Nashville buddy Lea Jane Berinati was in town, I set up a microphone in my stall shower so I could use it as a quiet sound booth for her. Unfortunately she backed against the shower faucet and got drenched. I never used that set-up again.)

My least favorite director really delivered a gut punch to our project just as Brick and Jim were leaving for rehearsals at a small theater in Deerfield Beach, Florida. He quit because he got a shot at directing a more important show. He left the directing to Brick, making him our leading actor, writer, and—now—director. That was too much for anyone, and although the show got good revues in the local *Broward News*, it was slaughtered in the *Miami New Times*, and *Cloverleaf Crisis* became a one-night wonder. Well, like they say, "That's show business." I ran back home to my jingles.

Here's one last "aside" to you, my readers. Our theater was in the ground floor of a building owned by a gynecologist. He used the second floor for his office and advertised his phone number on a sign outside the building. It was 1-800-<u>GYN</u>-O###.

Sadly, Brick died not too long after our show closed. I believe that he died thinking it wasn't fair that someone as talented as him had never cracked the big time—and was crushed when the show he had worked on for so long failed.

Chapter 11
I WAKE TO THE FACT THAT I AM AN OLDIE

OLDIES SHOWS

Oldies Shows are de rigueur for most artists who had hits in the 50s and 60s. They're great for the artists, who get a chance to resurrect careers that have past their prime, feel the love and respect which these special audiences have for them and at the same time earn some money from their music again. They're also a great opportunity for Oldies fans to see lots of their favorite artists singing lots of their favorite songs. Because I was off doing other things between and after my hits, I didn't get to perform at very many of these shows. But when I did perform, I often ran into the same artists—time after time, show after show. The shows' producers knew which artists were reliable and which ones weren't, so there was a group of artists who showed up all the time, to the delight of their fans who never could get enough of them.

In the summer of 1999, I got an email from Ken Keene, Frankie Ford's manager, asking me if I'd like to perform at Fabian's Concert and Golf Classic in North Carolina, a benefit for a charity that provided horse therapy for children with special needs. (Frankie Ford had a smash hit in 1959 with 'Sea Cruise', written by Huey "Piano" Smith, a legendary New Orleans R & B writer and performer.) My mother-in-law decorated a pair of jeans with gold braids and music notes down the legs and a sequined jukebox on the backside for this, my first Oldies Show. I enjoyed turning my back and showing off the jukebox to the audience. It always got a laugh. And I remember all the performers being driven from our hotel to the concert venue in antique cars, waving at the fans who lined the streets, cheering. I had forgotten how much fun it could be to sing in front of fans showing their love for my music, and I looked forward to my next oldies show.

Phil Welsh, who was in charge of Fabian's benefit, invited me back to North Carolina to perform at a concert in Fayetteville in 2004. I guess that I am an obsessive neurotic, because my wife remembers that I was the only performer there who warmed up by vocalizing before the concert.

Closer to home, in June 2000, I appeared at the Westbury Music Fair, a theater in the round with a revolving stage. I remember the Oldies fans reaching out to touch me as I walked down the aisle onto the stage. That was an expression of love and respect from fan to artist. I always picked out one woman at every appearance, and sang 'Roses Are Red' to her, because I expected tears when I sang the final verse and chorus;

> Is that your little girl? She looks a lot like you
> Someday some boy will write in her book too
> Roses Are Red, My Love. Violets are Blue
> Sugar is sweet, my love, but not as sweet as you

As you can imagine, keeping my eye on just one audience member was impossible to accomplish in a theater with a revolving stage. But I did the best that I could and got the result that I wanted. The woman that I had chosen cried (along with some other audience members). It was a successful performance. Unfortunately, a friend of mine was ejected from the theater for taking a short video of my appearance—strictly verboten at the theater. That video is now up on YouTube ("Paul Evans sings Happy Go Lucky Me"), thanks to him, Paul S. I'm only sorry that he didn't get to see the rest of the concert.

Last, but not least was a Lar Enterprises, Inc. concert at the Hauppauge High School in November 2005, a yearly two-day event that is still in existence. Although he wasn't the concert's host, Don

K. Reed, the well-known New York Oldies DJ, surprised me when he walked out on stage to introduce his good friend—me.

OLDIES AND THE INTERNET

I was on the Internet very early, making music and interacting with fans, due to three friends who were deeply involved with computer music, MS-DOS, and computers. First was Ned "Ebn" Liben, a computer music wizard, who had partnered with Robert Rosen to form the high-tech band Ebn-Ozn, which recorded 'AEIOU Sometimes Y', a club hit in 1983. I was in awe of what he could do with computer music and he helped me choose my computers and music equipment. Second was Ron Lockhart, a successful jingle writer and producer (Stanley Tools, Burger King, The Dime Savings Bank) who insisted that I should get on the Internet with my own site to promote my music career. He guided me through the difficult and scary (for me) process. Ron was also my computer guru and was always there with help when the inevitable computer related problems arose. Third was George Russo, who created The Wanderer, one of the first—if not the very first—Oldies Music site in 1992, when AOL controlled the majority of sites through its dial-up protocol. When the Internet opened up for the public in 1995, George

Paul Evans fan club card

decided to host his own site, thewanderers.com, and allow others to use his hosting service. He even allowed users to stream music from his site. That was 10 years before YouTube opened for business. Genius! I moved to George's server in 1997. That's when paulevans.com was created. And I don't remember any other singer/writer having a site on the Internet at that time.

My site opened up a world of new opportunities for me. Because I was on the Internet with "paulevans.com" so early, it allowed me to broaden my connection with the Oldies world of fans, disc jockeys, and concert producers who were looking for me but didn't know how or where to find me. Fan clubs had been an intermediary between fans and me, but now I could personally relate stories and provide information to people who were anxious to know about "their" artists who had created "their" music. After all, before rock 'n' roll, popular music was shared with all generations within families. But this was our music alone. Remember that I had been ostracized and banished from the family dinner table when I discovered this new sound. The older generation could like it or not, this was *our* music. And that's why there is such a big world of Oldies fans.

After I put up my site, I began to get emails from people who told me how much my music meant to them. Two particularly stand out in my mind. In one of them, a fan said that my music had made him feel as though I had been a member of his family for the past 30 years. The other email was from a young man who wrote to say that he had a disabling disease and the only thing that lifted his spirits was when he listened to my recording of 'Happy Go Lucky Me'. I've kept copies of both of those emails for whenever I've needed my own spirits raised. Most of the emails that I've received over the years have been to thank me for my songs that brought my fans back to their youth. They've made me aware that my music has made many people happy, and that's something I'll take to rock 'n' roll heaven with me—assuming that I get there.

I still receive emails about my music. While I was writing this book, I received a note from a group of Oldies lovers in the Netherlands, asking me for more details about my song 'Forget Me Not', co-written by Al Byron and recorded and taken to the Country charts by Steve Wariner in 1979—41 years ago! I've always made an effort to reply in person to the fan emails that I receive. Apparently, not many record artists do. In fact, I've received messages from fans who said they were "shocked" to get a reply from me.

I had an early experience that exposed the dark side of the Web to me. Very shortly after I put my email address up on my site, I received an email from a woman who said that Al Byron and I had not written 'Roses Are Red'. She said that her boyfriend had. However, she continued, she wasn't looking for any compensation for him, but would just like a letter confirming her story. Congratulations to me: that was my first email scam and I was savvy enough to not answer that email, one obviously not written by a fan.

I owe my appearance on Fabian's benefit concert to the Internet, when Ken Keene, Frankie Ford's manager, sent me an email saying that he'd been looking for me and was happy to have found my site. I had another concert booker find me through my site. That contact led to another concert, this time closer to home where so many of my friends showed up to whoop and holler. And again, going onto the Internet with my own site so early on has led to lasting relationships with disc jockeys—online and in person, and to countless interviews for both magazines and radio which have helped me to stay in touch with Oldies fans.

Bruce Morrow, best known as Cousin Brucie, has been an important New York DJ since I had my early hits. He hosts a yearly outdoor concert here in New York City, at the Feast of San Gennaro in an area of Manhattan called Little Italy. The audience is packed with Oldies fans. In fact, an entire block is cordoned off for Bruce. Well, a couple of years ago I performed at one of his shows. After the show, many people lined up to have me sign an autograph or to have their picture taken with me. At the end of the line was a young man, possibly not out of his teens. I asked him why he wanted to take my picture. His answer was, "My *grandmother* is a big fan of yours." Ouch.

I've also taken advantage of YouTube's presence on the Web and uploaded several musical videos:

"Paul Evans' Career":

Susan created this video. It traces my career in 7:14 minutes.

"Santa's Stuck Up in the Chimney"

The video now has over 3,000,000 views on YouTube. It was a big favorite with children and the song was performed at many a school's Christmas show.

"Happy Birthday, America (Independence Day)"

Another video created by Susan. This one for America's Independence Day. It was uploaded in "the bad old days", when YouTube restricted the size of your uploads. All the images that she used had to be downsized, which meant that the video appears a bit blurry. A French educational company wanted to use the video for French schools, but only if we could enhance the resolution of the pictures we used in the video. Unfortunately, the request came with a deadline that was impossible to meet, so Susan and I lost the opportunity to have our video shown in French écoles.

"Seven Little Girls"

I requested the video from Dick Clark and received it a few days later.

"Hello, This Is Joannie"

When England's Top of the Pops asked me to appear on their show, they also asked for a video. So I rushed into a studio to record Joannie just days before my trip to London.

Excerpts from my Ace (UK) CD, *Paul Evans.*

Once again, my wife's creation. We used the video to promote the CD.

"Paul Evans Sings Happy Go Lucky Me."

This is a short video because, as I've mentioned before, an usher stopped my friend from recording it and escorted him out of the theater for breaking the "No filming during the concert" rule.

One of Kent Cigarettes' "Happiness Is" commercials.

Thanks to Ben Bedridden who allowed me to share the video on my site.

The Internet has definitely changed the music industry. Several years ago, I saw the revival of *Jesus Christ Superstar* and was knocked out by the performance of the actor/singer who played the part of Judas. His performance was thrilling. Then my friend, sitting next to me, explained that the performer was the understudy to the original actor. I was astounded and thought, "How many wonderful talents there must be out in the world, just waiting for that one big break to bring them to the attention of the public."

The Internet has made it easier to get that attention—particularly in the pop music arena. Make a recording at home, upload a video of your recording to the Internet, and hope that it will attract a strong enough audience reaction for the music business to take notice.

But I still believe in what I learned at the Brill Building; the road to success starts with the song. Luck, how hard you're willing to work, and the people that you surround yourself with will determine the rest of your journey.

COMPILATION CDs

Compilation CDs are generally reissues of the best of the artists' repertoire all in one place. They've been a boon to artists and to their fans. The advantage to the fans is that it's an opportunity to purchase all of the best of their favorite's recordings in one CD instead of having to buy albums that sometimes lead with the hit of the moment and are filled up with "other" songs. It's true though, that with the capacity of today's CDs, compilations are often padded with those "other" songs. The advantage to the artists is that it keeps their songs visible. You just never know if someone in a position to use one of your songs in a film might hear it, or if an advertising agency's music producer might be looking for a copy of one of your songs.

I've had five compilations released. The first, *Paul Evans—The Fabulous Teens and Beyond*, was released in 1995 on Ace Records, a label known for reissuing fine quality American recordings. I was very happy when Ace requested a contract to release the CD, because they had a terrific distribution system that would make more of my songs available to fans. My wife and I were so enthused about having a compilation released on Ace Records that we decided to go to London to meet with some of the Ace staff to discuss the CD. I learned just what real Oldies fans were made out of in that nice English restaurant.

Susan and I sat down with John Broven and Rob Hughes and we quickly discovered that they knew more about my records than I did. Really! They talked about titles of songs that I had forgotten I had even written. They questioned me about co-writers on obscure recordings that I didn't remember. They debated who played the saxophone on different sessions for me, based solely on the musician's individual techniques. They knew more of the whos, hows, and whys of Paul Evans' career than I did.

I knew one thing that they didn't, though. They were curious as to how the sound of the water on 'Fish In The Ocean', the B-side of 'Happy Go Lucky Me', was made. C'mon, John. C'mon, Rob. There were no sequencers yet. It was just a musician blowing into a glass of water through a straw.

As I wrote before, I looked forward to my Ace release with a great deal of enthusiasm. It was well warranted. The package was filled with 28 tracks, all of them previously released, with the exception of my demo of 'Roses Are Red, My Love'. The CD had an insert filled with a great deal of information about my recording career. Roger Easterby, my Polydor publicist and big time Oldies enthusiast, wrote notes about my career, and I was given space to write notes from a more personal point of view. Rob Hughes wrote a very detailed discography, including each session's musicians and singers. I'd never seen anything like that discography before that Ace CD. And happily, working on the CD led to a life-long and rewarding friendship with John Broven and his wife Shelley.

Susan and I put the second compilation, *I Was a Part of the 50s,* together with help from the designer at Harry Hirsch's Digi-Rom Studio in 1998. We wanted to include some material that hadn't been part of the Ace compilation. I particularly wanted to include "I Was a Part of The 50's" which I released on my own label, S-Star

Records, and my first record ever, 'What Do You Know?', released on RCA Victor. (S-Star Records was created solely for this album project.)

Our CD included 18 tracks: all of my hit recordings, other recordings that Susan and I agreed "should have been hits", my demos of my hits by the Kalin Twins and Bobby Vinton, and an interview conducted by my friend Gary Theroux, a well-known radio personality and music historian. But even more fun than choosing the sides to include was the chance to write a thank you note to the musicians, singers, and others who had helped me throughout my career. We also included a letter from Dick Clark written specifically for the CD. As part of his letter Dick wrote, "Paul Evans made a distinctive mark on the music you and I have enjoyed over the years." In my thank you note to Dick I wrote, "I am a satisfied graduate of the Dick Clark School of Rock 'n' Roll."

In 2003, the third Paul Evans' compilation, *Happy Go Lucky Me,* was released on Castle Music, a subsidiary of the now defunct Sanctuary Records Group. Sam Szczepanski, the Special Markets Label Manager at Sanctuary, put it together with 28 tracks worth of my hit songs and other recordings that she chose. It also included several original demonstration records, including the two that were being held for Elvis Presley when he passed away. The insert was an unusually large, four-fold pullout that held an enormous amount of information and photos of yours truly. I was so proud of the CD that I travelled to London, where Sam, Roger Dopson and I did a promotion tour of lots of Oldies stations in and around London. A promotion trip for a compilation album was very unusual. But it was a fun trip. I travelled with a guitar and, I think, enhanced my reputation with a lot of terrific DJs who were surprised to have me show up and perform live on their shows.

Paul Evans is the title of my fourth compilation CD and the second to be released on Ace Records. Trevor Churchill, one of the owners of Ace, was always interested in ideas for artists' catalogs that would make an interesting compilation album. I called him and suggested that he might want to release my Kapp Records' album under the Ace banner. (The album had been released twice by Kapp under two different titles, *21 Years in a Tennessee Jail* and *Another Town-Another Jail.*) However, there just weren't enough songs in the album to interest Trevor. Susan saved the CD idea when she suggested that my early Carlton album *Folk Songs Of Many Lands* would fit nicely with the country music of *Another Town – Another Jail* and Trevor agreed. Two albums released on one CD for fans and collectors, thanks to my wife and Trevor Churchill's Ace Records.

The fifth compilation was released in 2020. *Paul Evans—Seven Little Girls* is a two-CD set from Jasmine Records that contains all of my releases from 1957 to 1962. Singles, both A- and B-sides, from RCA Victor, Decca, Atco, Guaranteed, Carlton, and Kapp Records, and albums from Carlton and Guaranteed. That comes to 66 tracks. I love what this CD does for me. It reminds me of the beginnings of a lifelong career filled with music. In fact, because it includes recordings from my pre 'Seven Little Girls' days with RCA Victor, Decca, and Atco Records, it's allowed me to once again hear my earliest recordings. I hadn't been able to listen to them since I traded up from my record player to my CD disc player—and had forgotten some of the titles that this compilation has now brought back to me. To be quite honest, some of those records make me cringe and say to myself, *What in the world was I thinking?* And yet, when I listen back to the recordings, others make me wonder, *What made this song unworthy of radio play and why wasn't it a hit?*

Despite the fact that downloading and streaming sites have made music easily available, somehow companies like Ace and Jasmine Records are still in the business of producing good-quality compilation CDs and keeping fans and recording artists happy.

WORKING MY MUSIC

A few years ago I realized that my songs' futures depended on syncs; the use of songs in television shows, films, video games, commercials, etc. Until then I had been on the receiving end of requests for the use of my songs, but those requests had been getting fewer and fewer. Unfortunately my catalog was getting older and I didn't have the know-how or the contacts needed to promote my songs to that market.

Kent Cigarettes had requested the license for 'Happiness Is' from Mills Music for a three-year plus television campaign. John Waters was determined to use 'Happy Go Lucky Me' and had his staff pursue the record until they found it. The UK's giant Sainsbury's grocery chain knew that George Formby's cover of 'Happy Go Lucky Me' would work in a very successful Christmas television campaign.

Here are some more of my songs that were requested by users and licensed for films, TV, or commercials, without my having to do anything but pick up my phone. I guess that you could say that they fell into my lap:

'Live Young', in the film *Palm Springs Weekend.*
'Let's Pretend', Lulu's version, in the long-time British hit *Ab Fab.*
'Let's Pretend', Lulu's version, in the Australian film *Home Song Stories.*
'Our World', in the major American TV series *Mad Men.*
'When', in the Rob Reiner film *Flipped.*
'When', in *The Singing Detective*, starring Robert Downey, Jr.
'When', a commercial for the English furniture company, Wren.
'Seven Little Girls Sitting in the Back Seat', in a Mainland Chinese film, *Summer Palace.*

But rather than just sitting back and waiting for my telephone to ring, I made a very difficult decision. I'd have to give up control of my babies—my songs—to someone who could actively seek out sync licenses. (I've written and recorded two songs about my songs as my children: 'Half Man – Half Music' and 'All My Children'.) However, difficult or not, I realized that hearing my songs in theaters and on the TV screen was better than admiring them while they sat on my record and CD shelves. It was the correct decision. Since taking on an administrator for my copyrights—Mark Fried and his crews at Spirit and Mojo Music—I've had 'Happy Go Lucky Me' used in Hulu's film *11.22.63* and 'Happiness Is' used for a Christmas campaign for the e-commerce giant eBay. The French version of my Elvis recording 'I Gotta Know' ('Je T'Aime Trop') was used and then picked up for a second run on a popular commercial for Intermarché, the French supermarket chain. And to my delight, 'When' was used on one of my favorite television series, *Mrs. Maisel.*

EPILOGUE

A RIDE ON A MUSICAL MERRY-GO-ROUND

Readers of this book might have gotten the impression that I've reeled around the music business from here to there, directionless. I don't think that's correct. I believe that once I tasted success at the Brill Building, and realized that I was a part of the Brill's songwriting community and could express myself creatively through music—writing and singing—my plan was to be wherever music took me. And, after some 63 music-filled years, wherever it is still taking me.

Some of my career was successful, and some mistakes were made along the way, but my life has been a musical merry-go-round ride and that's been a gift of the gods. From the day I stepped into the Brill Building until the time that I felt I was part of the music world and still today, I've lived in a grand and always exciting world of heroes and scoundrels. I tip my hat to the writers, musicians and singers who rose from the pack to the top of the list of winners and losers.

When I look back at my music career, it does remind me a bit of a couple of lines of Sinatra's big hit, 'That's Life', written by Dean Kay and Kelly Gordon:

> I've been a puppet, a pauper, a pirate, a poet,
> A pawn and a king.

Well, I've been a soloist, group singer, pop and country music songwriter, pop singer, country singer, jazz singer, demo singer, a jingle producer, writer and singer, off-Broadway show writer, television performer, stage performer, ship singer, headliner and a background performer. Some of these stops along the pathway of my life just fell into my lap. Some lasted and others were short-lived. And when one area started to slip, I'd look around to find a new music challenge that I thought I would enjoy and where I thought I could succeed. There were failures and disappointments as well as successes. But it was all good. My life has been filled with music, I've made good friends, had good partners, and I've always had a couple of bucks in my pockets. That's been a life well lived, a musical trip that started at home with a musical family, encouraging friends, a little talent and a little luck. Like a yellow brick road, my life's path was laid out in front of me once I stepped into the Brill Building.

I WAS A PART OF THE 50's
Words and Music by Paul Evans

I was a part of the 50's
That was a time, but now it's gone
I Moondogged with Alan Freed when Rock 'n' Roll was born
Well it was hot and if you missed it—you missed a lot

Yes, I was a part of the 50's
Oh, yes I was, and don't you know
That I saw half of Elvis Presley on the old *Ed Sullivan Show*
Can you believe—that was 60* years ago

How well I remember Philadelphia, PA.
The capital of all the dance parties across the U.S.A.

And I was a part of the 50's
I sang a song that got ahead
I sang: 'Seven Little Girls Sittin' In The Back Seat Kissin' and a-Huggin' with Fred'
It hit the charts and forever it will live in my heart

Goodbye Perry Como, Dinah Shore and Doris Day
Hello Elvis, Hello Little Richard, Rock 'n' Roll is here to stay, Hey

I was a part of the 50's
I sang a song that got ahead
I sang 'Seven Little Girls Sittin' In The Back Seat
Kissin' and a-Huggin' with Fred'

It hit the charts and forever it will live in my heart
I was a part of the 50's
(Girls) We were a part of it too
(All) If you weren't part of it, deep in the heart of it
We feel sorry for you

Shoo-wop shoo wop, Shoo wop shoo wop, Shoo
waddy-i-o)

*The original lyric about Elvis Presley on the old *Ed Sullivan Show* was "40 years ago". Time has a nasty habit of marching on.

... AND ONE FINAL NOTE

I began my book-writing career in March 2020, the year of the COVID-19 virus. I wrote four to five hours a day, six days a week, until sometime in November when McNidder & Grace approved a final draft. But I have no complaints. Writing *Happy Go Lucky Me* probably saved my sanity and maybe even my marriage. Okay, you might call it hyperactivity (although I prefer exuberance), but without the book to write, I certainly would have wandered around my New York City apartment shouting, "I have nothing to do! I have nothing to do!" I did have something to do; I had a book to write. Lucky Susan, lucky neighbors, and lucky me!

It has been my great pleasure to collect my thoughts and write this book.

Appendix 1
PAUL EVANS' DISCOGRAPHY

USA and UK Releases
Compiled by Rob Hughes
Additions by Tony Wilkinson and Paul Evans'
Comments by Paul

My first record release

RCA VICTOR

#6808 (1957)	**What Do You Know?** (Paul Evans)
	Dorothy (Lincoln Chase)
#6924 (1957)	**Looking For A Sweetie** (Paul Evans)
	Any Little Thing (Jack Reardon/Sid Jacobson
#6992 (1957)	**Caught** (Clyde Otis/James Deliston)
	Poor Broken Heart (Paul Evans)

DECCA RECORDS

#30680 (1958)	**I Think About You All The Time** (Paul Evans/Jack Reardon)
	Oh! No (Paul Evans/Jack Reardon)

Decca Records had five hits in the Top 100 in the summer of '58. 'I Think About You All The Time' was their sixth best seller. They neglected to let me know that it hit the charts in Canada. I found this out when some fans requested the song while I was playing a hop in Canada.

ATCO RECORDS

#6138 (1959) **At My Party** (Paul Evans/Jack Reardon)
Beat Generation (Paul Evans/Woody Harris)

#6170 (1960) **Long Gone** (Paul Evans/Jack Reardon)
Mickey, My Love (Prescott, Coldin,Russell)

GUARANTEED RECORDS

#200 (1959) **Seven Little Girls** (Bob Hilliard/ Lee Pockriss)
Worshipping An Idol (Bob Hilliard/ Lee Pockriss)

'Seven Little Girls' was released under the name Paul Evans and the Curls.

#205 (1960) **Midnight Special** (Arranged by Paul Evans)
Since I Met You Baby (Ivory Joe Hunter)

An arrangement of an American folk song about the legend of the Midnight Special: if it shone its light on you in your prison cell at the stroke of midnight, you'd soon be released. I first did this song live while traveling on the road with the Bobby Comstock Band ('Tennessee Waltz').

#208 (1960) **Happy-Go-Lucky-Me** (Al Byron/ Paul Evans)
Fish In The Ocean (Bubbly Bum Bum) (P. Evans/ J. Krondes)

'Fish In the Ocean' was supposed to be the A-side from this recording session. (One of Guaranteed Record's executives blew into a water glass with a straw to produce the "bubbly, bum bum" sound.) Harder than singing on 'Happy-Go-Lucky Me' was laughing on it. When the record was covered in a K-Tel album knock-off of the top 10 hits of the day, one performer sang the song and another laughed on it.

#210 (1960) **The Brigade Of Broken Hearts** (Fred Tobias/Clint Ballard)
Twins (Aaron Schroeder, J. Leslie McFarland)

#213 (1960)
Hushabye, Little Guitar (Paul Evans/ Matt Williams)
Blind Boy (Paul Evans/Al Byron)

LP 1000 (1960)
PAUL EVANS SINGS THE FABULOUS TEENS
I'm In Love Again (Antoine Domino/ Dave Bartholomew)
Hambone Rock (Red Saunders/ Leon Washington)
Over The Mountain, Across The Sea (Rex Garvin)
Tutti Frutti (Richard Penniman/ Dorothy LaBostrie/Joe Lubin)
Butterfly (Anthony September)
Midnight Special (Arranged by Paul Evans)
Slippin' And Slidin' (Penniman/Bocage/ Collins/Smith)
Honey Love (Gerald Wexler/ Clyde McPhatter)
I'm Walkin' (Anton Domino/ Dave Bartholomew)
Since I Met You Baby (Ivory Joe Hunter)
60 Minute Man (Billy Ward/Rose Marks)
The Fool (Lee Hazlewood)

LONDON RECORDS (UK)

#8968 (1959)
Seven Little Girls (Lee Pockriss, Bob Hiliard)
Worshipping An Idol (Lee Pockriss, Bob Hilliard)

#9045 (1960)
Midnite Special (Arranged by Paul Evans)
Since I Met You Baby (Ivory Joe Hunter)

#9129 (1960)
Happy-Go-Lucky-Me (Paul Evans, Al Byron)
Fish In The Ocean (P. Evans/ J. Krondes)

#9183 (1960)	**The Brigade Of Broken Hearts** (Fred Tobias/Clint Ballard) **Twins** (Aaron Schroeder, J. Leslie McFarland)
#9239 (1960)	**Hushabye, Little Guitar** (Paul Evans/ Matt Williams) **Blind Boy** (Paul Evans/Al Byron)
#9636 (1962)	**Gilding The Lily** (Paul Evans/Al Byron) **The Bell That Couldn't Jingle** (Burt Bacharach, Larry Kusik)
#9770 (1963)	**Ten Thousand Tears** (Allan Roberts) **Even Tan** (Paul Evans/Jack Reardon)
#10340(1971)	**Think Summer** (Paul Evans/Paul Parnes) **For Old Times Sake** (Evans/Parnes/ Ulvaeus/Anderson)

LP 2248 (1960) ***PAUL EVANS SINGS THE FABULOUS TEENS***

The cover of this LP is the same as Guaranteed LP 1000. Without adding the titles to the cover, London Records added two tracks to the LP, 'Seven Little Girls' and 'Worshipping An Idol'.

Seven Little Girls (Lee Pockriss/ Bob Hilliard)
Slippin' And Slidin' (Penniman/Bocage/ Collins/Smith)
I'm Walkin' (Anton Domino/ Dave Bartholomew)
Butterfly (Anthony September)
Since I Met You Baby (Ivory Joc Hunter)
60 Minute Man (Billy Ward/Rose Marks)
I'm In Love Again (Antoine Domino/ Dave Bartholomew)
Over The Mountain, Across The Sea (Rex Garvin)
The Fool (Lee Hazlewood)
Honey Love (Gerald Wexler/ Clyde McPhatter)

	Hambone Rock (Red Saunders/ Leon Washington) **Tutti Frutti** (Richard Penniman/ Dorothy LaBostrie/Joe Lubin) **Midnight Special** (Arranged by Paul Evans) **Worshipping An Idol** (Lee Pockriss, Bob Hilliard)

CARLTON RECORDS

#539 (1961)	**Show Folk** (Ellis/Stillman) **I Love To Make Love To You** (Allen, Hilliard)
#543 (1961)	**After The Hurricane** (Paul Evans, Al Byron) **Not Me** (Gloria Regney)
#554 (1961)	**This Pullover** (Stellman, Migliacci. Meccia) **Just Because I Love You** (Mosely, Murray)
#558 (1961)	**Sisal Twine** (Evans, Karen) **Over The Mountain, Across The Sea** (Rex Garvin)
LP 129 (1961)	***HEAR PAUL EVANS IN YOUR HOME TONIGHT*** **Seven Little Girls** (Lee Pockriss/ Bob Hilliard) **Happy-Go-Lucky-Me** (Paul Evans/ Al Byron) **Blind Boy** (Paul Evans/Al Byron) **Why** (Paul Evans/ Paul Parnes) **Long Live Love** (Paul Evans/ Jack Reardon) **Worshipping An Idol** (Lee Pockriss/ Bob Hilliard) **The Brigade Of Broken Hearts** (Fred Tobias/Clint Ballard)

Twins (Aaron Schroeder, J. Leslie McFarland)
Fire In My Soul (Evans/Sexter)
Fish In The Ocean (P. Evans/ J. Krondes)
King Of Broken Hearts (Paul Evans/ Al Byron)
Hushabye, Little Guitar (Paul Evans/ Matt Williams)

LP 130 (1961) ***FOLKS SONGS OF MANY LANDS***
Passing Through (Arrangement by Paul Evans)
Wee Cooper O'Fife (Arrangement by Paul Evans)
Buckeye Jim (Arrangement by Paul Evans)
Kevin Barry (Arrangement by Paul Evans)
Tzena Tzena (Issachar Miron/Mitchell Parish/Yehiel Haggiz)
Los Cuatros Generales (Arrangement by Paul Evans)
Mister Hangman (Arrangement by Paul Evans)
British Grenadiers (Arrangement by Paul Evans)
Wayfarin' Stranger (Arrangement by Paul Evans)
Wearing Of The Green (Arrangement by Paul Evans)
Colorado Trail (Arrangement by Paul Evans)
Samuel Hall (Arrangement by Paul Evans)
Golden Vanity (Arrangement by Paul Evans)
Pig And The Inebriate (Arrangement by Paul Evans)

The Bomb (Arrangement by Paul Evans)
Crucified My Lord (James Whitbourn)
Poor Boy (Arrangement by Paul Evans)

I remember Carlton Record executives arguing whether or not "Yankee, Russian, White or Tan, Lord, a Man is Just a Man" (from the song 'Passing Through') was too controversial (for the times) to be released in a pop album.

KAPP RECORDS

#473 (1962)	**Feelin' No Pain** (Burt Bacharach, Bob Hilliard)
	A Picture Of You (Oakman/Beveridge)
#486 (1962)	**D-Darling** (Leslie Bricusse)
	Gonna Build A Mountain (Leslie Bricusse/AnthonyNewley)
#499 (1962)	**Gilding The Lily** (Paul Evans/Al Byron)
	The Bell That Couldn't Jingle (Larry Kusik/Burt Bacharach)
#520 (1963)	**We've Got Something On You** (Kaufman/Anthony)
	What Are The Lips Of Janet (Shuman/ Carr)
#527 (1963)	**Ten Thousand Tears** (Allen Roberts)
	Even Tan (Jack Reardon/Paul Evans)
#567 (1963)	**I'm Gonna Build A Girl** (Evans/Tobias)
	Two Different Things (Evans/Tobias)
LP 3346 (1964)	***21 YEARS IN A TENNESSEE JAIL*** (With the Rocky Mount Ramblers)
	Ninety-Nine Years (Bill Anderson)
	Shackles And Chains (Arrangement by Paul Evans)
	The Prisoner's Song (Arrangement by Paul Evans)
	Another Town – Another Jail (Paul Evans/Jack Reardon)
	Allentown Jail (Irving Gordon)

	I Got Stripes (Johnny Cash/ Charlie Williams)
	Twenty-One Years (Arrangement by Paul Evans)
	In The Jailhouse Now (Jimmy Rogers)
	Marie, Marie (Gilbert Becaud/ Lee Pockriss/Paul Vance)
	Betty & Dupree's Blues (Paul Evans)
	Columbus Stockade Blues (Paul Evans)
	John Hardy (Paul Evans)
Bonus Track	**Midnite Special** (Arranged by Paul Evans)

LONDON AMERICAN RECORDS (UK)

#RE-R 1349 (1962)	**A Picture of You** (Oakman/Beveridge)
	Feelin' No Pain (Burt Bacharach, Bob Hilliard)
	Gonna Build a Mountain (Leslie Bricusse/AnthonyNewley)
	D-Darling (Leslie Bricusse)

EPIC RECORDS

#9728 (1964)	**Bewitched** (with Mimi Evans) (Jack Keller/Howie Greenfield)
	I Think I'm Gonna Kill Myself (with Mimi Evans) (Buddy Knox)
#9751 (1964)	**Gina Marina Petunia** (Rudy Clark)
	Little Miss Tease (Dave Burgess)
#9842 (1965)	**Always Thinking Of The Roses** (Paul Evans)
	I Wonder What To Do (Paul Evans/ Paul Parnes)

COLUMBIA RECORDS

#44472 (1968)	**One Red Rose** (Paul Evans/Paul Parnes)
	Bound To Silence (Paul Evans)

LAURIE RECORDS

#3571 (1971) **Think Summer** (Paul Evans/Paul Parnes)
For Old Times Sake (Evans/Parnes/Ulvacus/Anderson)

#3581 (1971) **The Man In The Rowboat** (Paul Evans)
Here We Go 'Round Again (Paul Evans)

#3614 (1973) **Natural Cotton – Natural Man (vocal)** (P. Evans/P. Parnes)
Natural Cotton – Natural Man (instrumental) (Evans/Parnes)

This was originally written as a jingle and was released under the name "Eli Whitney". The instrumental was released under the name of "The Eli Whitney Brass Band". I'd forgotten about this record. Thanks to Jim Stone of Big Band Swing *for remembering.*

RANWOOD RECORDS

#928 (1972) **Try It, You'll Like** It (Charles Randolph Grean)
We Liked It (Charles Randolph Grean)

DOT RECORDS

17463 (1973) **Do You Remember** (Paul Evans)
That's What Loving You Is All About (Evans/Michlin/Hatcher)

MERCURY RECORDS

73499 (1974) **But I Was Born In New York City** (Bob Kessler/Paul Evans)
Just As Long As You Are There (Paul Evans)

73650 (1975) **All My Children** (Paul Evans)
Move In With Me (Paul Evans)

BIG TREE RECORDS

16050 (1975) **Happy Birthday, America** (Paul Evans/Jimmy Krondes)

You Made Me Over (Paul Evans/ Kiev Ginsberg)

MUSICOR RECORDS

6305 (1977) **If I Had My Life To Live Over** (Paul Parnes/Paul Evans)
Roses Are Red Medley

The Medley consisted of four songs: 'Roses are Red' (A. Byron/P. Evans), 'Red Roses for a Blue Lady' (S. Tepper/R. Bennett), 'Rambling Rose' (N. Sherman/J. Sherman) and 'Roses Always Remember' (H. David/P. Evans)

SPRING RECORDS

#183 (1978) **Hello, This Is Joannie** (Fred Tobias/ Paul Evans)
Lullaby Tissue Paper Company (Bryan Wells/Paul Evans)

A Country Billboard *Top 40 record, 'Joannie' went to #1 on every big-city country station in the U.S. and went to #6 on the British pop charts. This was my first record produced in Nashville, TN.*

#187 (1978) **Down At The Bluebird** (Marty Kupersmith/Paul Evans)
I'm Givin' Up My Baby (Fred Tobias/ Paul Evans)

#193 (1979) **Disneyland Daddy** (Paul Evans)
Build An Ark (Paul Evans)

SPRING RECORDS (UK)

#2066932 (1978) **Hello, This Is Joannie** (Fred Tobias/ Paul Evans)
Lullaby Tissue Paper Company (Bryan Wells/Paul Evans)

#39 (1979) **What's A Nice Guy Like Me Doing In A Place Like This** (Paul Evans/ Martin Kupersmith)
Build An Ark (Paul Evans)

POLYDOR RECORDS (UK)

#39 (1979) — **What's A Nice Guy Like Me Doing In A Place Like This** (Paul Evans/ Martin Kupersmith)
Build An Ark (Paul Evans)

'What's A Nice Guy' was initially issued in the UK on Spring #39 (see SPRING RECORDS [UK] above). When Polydor folded Spring, they kept the release available on the parent label.

LP 1008 (1979) — *HELLO, THIS IS PAUL EVANS*
Build An Ark (Paul Evans)
Rosemaria (Paul Evans/Bruce Pollock)
Hello, This Is Joannie (Fred Tobias/ Paul Evans)
Disneyland Daddy (Paul Evans)
Half Man, Half Music (Paul Evans/ Bob Alan)
What's A Nice Guy Like Me Doing In A Place Like This? (Paul Evans/ Martin Kupersmith)
Lullaby Tissue Paper Company (Bryan Wells/Paul Evans)
Mack The Knife (Kurt Weill)
I'm Giving Up My Baby (Fred Tobias/ Paul Evans)
The First Time I've Had Second Thoughts. (Paul Evans/Kiev Ginsberg)

RCA RECORDS (UK)

#5260 (1980) — **Good Neighbour** (Paul Evans)
An Angel With A Broken Wing (Paul Evans/Larry Rush)

CINNAMON RECORDS

#804 (1980) — **One Night Led To Two** (Bob Alan/ Paul Evans)

Hangin' Out And Hangin' In
(Paul Parnes/Paul Evans)

GARDEN OF EDEN RECORDS

#CD-2100 (1993) **"WILLIE'S SUNG WITH EVERYONE (BUT ME)"**
Willie's Sung With Everyone (But Me)
(Paul Evans)
Santa's Stuck Up In The Chimney
(Paul Parnes/Paul Evans)
The Beautiful Grass Of Kentucky
(Al Byron/Paul Evans
The Yodelin' Jazzman (with Group 5ive)
(Paul Evans)

WIZWORKS RECORDS

#WW1110CD (2002) ***ROSES ARE RED, MY LOVE***
Build An Ark (Paul Evans)
To Make You Feel My Love (Bob Dylan)
Dot-Com Blues (Jimmy Wisner/Joe McMahon Jr.)
Roses Are Red (My Love) (Al Byron/Paul Evans)
Rosemaria (Paul Evans/Bruce Pollock)
When (Jack Reardon/Paul Evans)
By An Oleander Tree (Joe McMahon, Jr.)
Hangin' Out And Hangin' In
(Paul Evans/Paul Parnes)
Good Neighbor (Paul Evans)
Angel with A Broken Wing (Paul Evans/Larry Rush)
Weekend Daddy (Paul Evans)
Amazing Grace (Trad. New lyrics by Paul Evans)

FSA RECORDS

(July, 2006) **'HAPPY BIRTHDAY, AMERICA'**
A remixed and remastered version of the song, originally issued for the American Bicentennial in1976.
(December, 2006) **'SANTA'S STUCK UP IN THE CHIMNEY'**
A remixed and remastered version of the song.

COMPILATION CDs

ACE RECORDS (UK)

#CD 551 (1995) ***THE FABULOUS TEENS AND BEYOND***
Midnite Special / Hushabye, Little Guitar / I'm In Love Again
Hambone Rock / Over The Mountain, Across The Sea /Tutti Frutti / Butterfly Slippin' And Slidin' / Honey Love / I'm Walkin'
Since I Met You Baby / 60 Minute Man / The Fool / Seven Little Girls
Worshipping An Idol / Happy-Go-Lucky-Me / Fish In The Ocean
The Brigade Of Broken Hearts / Blind Boy / Twins / After The Hurricane Just Because I Love You / Show Folk / Why / Roses Are Red
Disneyland Daddy / Willie's Sung With Everyone (But Me)
Hello, This Is Joannie.

S-STAR RECORDS (USA)

#CD 1214 (1998) ***I WAS PART OF THE 50s***
I Was Part Of The 50's / Seven Little Girls / Midnite Special / Honey Love
Happy-Go-Lucky-Me / The Brigade Of Broken Hearts / After The Hurricane
Hushabye, Little Guitar / Happy Birthday, America / Hello, This Is Joannie
Hangin' Out And Hangin' In / Bye Bye Love
Willie's Sung With Everyone (But Me) / I Gotta Know (*live*)
What Do You Know? / Roses Are Red / When
An interview and reprise of I Was Part Of The 50's.

CASTLE RECORDS (UK)

#CRRCD715 (April, 2003) ***HAPPY GO LUCKY ME – THE PAUL EVANS SONGBOOK***
What Do You Know? / Cry, Baby, Cry, / Good Good Thing
Seven Little Girls (Sitting in the Back Seat)
Since I Met You Baby / 60 Minute Man / Midnight Special / The Fool
Happy-Go-Lucky Me / Twins / Hushabye, Little Guitar / This Pullover
If I Had My Live To Live Over / Hello, This Is Joannie / I Gotta Know
When / If There Were No Moon / Johnny Will / Something Blue
Roses Are Red (My Love) / Worried Guy / You Won't See Me Anymore
Happiness Is / The Next Step Is Love / Tender Moments / Quiet Desperation
Stuart Coleman Interview / I Was a Part of the 50's

ACE RECORDS (UK)

#CDTOP 1367 (2013) ***PAUL EVANS***
Consists of two formerly released albums, Carlton's *FOLK SONGS OF MANY LANDS* and Kapp Records' *21 YEARS IN A TENNESSEE JAIL*

JASMINE RECORDS (UK)

#JASCD 870 (2020) **PAUL EVANS – SITTING IN THE BACK SEAT**
Complete Masters, 1957–1962 (66 Tracks from RCA Victor, Decca, Atco and Kapp Records.)

Notes:

1) Kapp LP #3346, *21 Years In A Tennessee Jail* was also released as *Another Town, Another Jail.*
2) Unissued tracks from the first signing with RCA Records in 1956/57 are: 'Cry Baby Cry', 'Give Me A Woman', 'Good Good

Thing', 'Be My Baby Again', 'Baby Come Home' and 'Let Me Know'.

3) This discography has concentrated on USA and UK releases only. Paul Evans has had records released throughout the world.

Appendix 2
PAUL'S SONGS RECORDED BY OTHER ARTISTS

Compiled by Susan Evans

Song	Artist	Co-writer	Year	Record Label
2001	Ed Ames	Paul Parnes	1969	RCA Victor
All Of My Life	The Metros	Jimmy Krondes	1958	Just Records
Are You Kissing More Now (And Enjoying It Less)	Homer & Jethro	Fred Tobias	1962	RCA Victor
Are You Kissing More Now (And Enjoying It Less)	Bill & Boyd	Fred Tobias	1962	Philips Records Australia
Batch Of Love	Don Rondo	Helene & Jack Polon	1959	Roulette
Birthdays Have A Way Of Coming 'Round	Robin Grean	No Co-writer	1972	Ranwood
Blue River #95 on Billboard Hot 100 chart #22 on U.K. charts	Elvis Presley	Fred Tobias	1965	RCA Victor
Build An Ark	The New Gaither Vocal Band	No Co-writer	1984	Dayspring

Song	Artist	Co-writer	Year	Record Label
Build An Ark	The Cathedrals	No Co-writer	1984	Riversong
Build An Ark Included in their Grammy award winning CD, *Lovin' Life*	Gaither Vocal Band	No Co-writer	2008	Gaither Music Group
Build An Ark	Guy Penrod	No Co-writer	2017	Gaither Music Group
Buy, Buy, Buy	The Geezinslaw Brothers	No Co-writer	1966	Capitol
Carol Made Her Choice	The Bachelors	Fred Tobias	1963	Decca
Carol Made Her Choice	Max Falcon	Fed Tobias	1963	Fraternity Records
Christmas, Country Style	Johnny Tillotson	Paul Parnes	1966	MGM
Cindy Is Gone	Bob Conrad	Fred Tobias	1962	Warner Bros
Comfortable (With Her)	Peter Lawford	Paul Parnes	1969	Bravo
Concerto For Knives, Forks, Spoons And One Soup Ladle	Charles Randolph Grean Sounde	Paul Parnes	1969	Ranwood
Congratulations, I Guess	Jerry Vale	Paul Parnes	1969	Columbia
Congratulations, I Guess	Jane Morgan	Paul Parnes	1969	RCA
Country Boy In The Army, A	Dorsey Brunette	Fred Tobias	1962	Dot Records
Daddy Couldn't Get Me One Of Those	Helen Shapiro	Fred Tobias	1963	Capitol Records U.K.
Daddy Couldn't Get Me One Of Those	Dodie Stevens	Fred Tobias	1963	Imperial
Dix-A-Billy B-side of "I Cried a Tear"	LaVern Baker	Woody Harris, Jack Reardon	1958	Atlantic

Song	Artist	Co-writer	Year	Record Label
Dix-A-Billy	Buddy Brooks AKA Barry Mann	Woody Harris, Jack Reardon	1958	Eagle Records
Drop Me A Line	Karl Hammel Jr.	Jimmy Krondes	1963	Laurie Records
Everything's The Same	Wes Voight AKA Chip Black	Woody Harris	1959	King Records
Fallin' In Love	The Lindsey Triplets	Fred Tobias	1959	Top Rank
Feelin' #14 on Billboard Adult Contemporary chart	Marilyn Maye	Paul Parnes	1968	RCA Victor
Field Of Flowers	Vernon Oxford	Al Bryon	1967	RCA Victor
Field Of Flowers	Delia Bell & Bill Grant	Al Byron	1984	Rounder Records
Followed Closely By My Tear Drops #15 on Billboard Country chart	Hank Locklin	Fred Tobias	1964	RCA Victor
Forget Me Not #49 Billboard Country chart	Steve Warnier	Al Byron	1979	RCA
Forget Me Not	Kikki Danielsson	Al Byron	1981	Mariann Records Sweden
Forget Me Not (Förgät Mig Ej)	Anne Kihlström	Al Byron, Alf Robertson	1984	Scranta Swedish
Fun	Tranquility Base	Paul Parnes	1970	RCA
Fun	Ronnie Prophet	Paul Parnes	1973	RCA
Funniest Thing I Ever Heard, The	Jimmy Dean	Larry Kusik	1963	Columbia
Girls Grow Up Faster Than Boys	Jimmy Griffith	Fred Tobias	1962	Reprise
Going, Going, Gone	Bonnie Guitar	Paul Parnes	1968	Dot Records
Good Good Thing	Four Voices	Jack Reardon	1960	Columbia

Song	Artist	Co-writer	Year	Record Label
Hand A Handkerchief To Helen #41 on U.K. charts	Susan Maughan	Fred Tobias	1963	Philips Records U.K.
Happiness Called	Carol Hall	Fred Tobias	1962	Columbia
Happiness Is #26 on Billboard Adult Contemporary chart	The Ray Coniff Singers	Paul Parnes	1966	Columbia
Happiness Is #28 on Billboard Adult Contemporary chart	Count Basie with the Alan Copeland Singers	Paul Parnes	1966	Columbia
Happiness Is #32 on Billboard Adult Contemporary chart	Joe Sherman	Paul Parnes	1966	Cameo
Happiness Is	The Mariachi Brass with Chet Baker	Paul Parnes	1966	World Pacific
Happiness Is	Clark Terry & Chico O'Farrill	Paul Parnes	1966	Impulse! Records
Happiness Is	Hugo Winterhalter & His Orchestra	Paul Parnes	1966	Musicor Records
Happiness Is	Lenny Dee (Organist)	Paul Parnes	1966	Decca
Happy Go Lucky Me #40 on U.K. charts	George Forrnby	Al Byron	1960	PYE Records U.K.
Happy-Go-Lucky Me	Frank Ifield	Al Byron	1960	Columbia U.K.
Happy Go Lucky Me	Otto Brandenburg	Al Byron,	1960	Odeon Denmark
Happy Go Lucky Me	Buddy Cagle	Al Byron	1970	United Artists
Harry's Harem	Cee Joy	Fred Tobias	1963	Warner Brothers
Here We Go Round Again	Leonard Nimoy	Paul Parnes	1968	Dot Records

Song	Artist	Co-writer	Year	Record Label
Here We Go Round Again	Vince Hill	Paul Parnes	1970	EMI Columbia
Here We Go Round Again	Sergio Franchi	Paul Parnes	1970	United Artists
Hole In My Heart	George Owens	Paul Parnes	1966	RCA Victor
How Did It Get So Late So Early	Wayne Newton	Paul Parnes	1965	Capitol
I Can't Help This Feeling I Feel	John Davidson	Paul Parnes	1966	Columbia
I Could Conquer The World #104 on Billboard Top 200 chart	The Shevelles	No Co-writer	1964	World Artists/ United Artists
I Could Conquer The World	Don Charles	No Co-writer	1965	HMV U.K.
If I Had My Life To Live Over	Slim Whitman	Paul Parnes	1981	Epic
I Gotta Know	Cliff Richard & the Shadows	Matt Williams	1959	Columbia U.K.
I Gotta Know #20 on Billboard Hot 100 chart; B-side of "Are You Lonesome Tonight"	Elvis Presley	Matt Williams	1960	RCA Victor
I Gotta Know (Je T'aime Trop)	Eddy Mitchell and Les Chaussettes Noires	M. Williams, E. Mitchell, J. Dambrois	1961	Barclay France
I Gotta Know	Bobby Vee and the Crickets	M. Williams	1962	Liberty
I Gotta Know (Professor De Amor)	Roberto Carlos	Matt Williams, Marcos Moran	1963	CBS Portugal
I Never Loved You Anyway	Johnny Tillotson	Paul Parnes	1965	MGM
I Search For Tomorrow	Leonard Nimoy	Paul Parnes	1969	Dot Records

Song	Artist	Co-writer	Year	Record Label
I'd Like Her To Be	Bill Courtney	David Fleischhacker	1959	RCA Victor
I'm In This Town For Good	Johnny Duncan	Paul Parnes	1968	Columbia
I'm Gonna Settle Down	Eddie Fontaine	Fred Tobias	1963	Warner Brothers
I've Seen Better Days	Johnny Tillotson	Paul Parnes	1965	MGM
In The Wind	John Gary	Spencer Michlin	1972	Victor
It Takes Two	Bobby Rydell	Paul Parnes	1965	Capital
It Takes Two	Ray Coniff & the Singers	Paul Parnes	1966	Columbia
Jigsaw Puzzle	Bobby Helms	Paul Parnes	1966	Kapp Records
Jigsaw Puzzle	CL & the Pictures	Paul Parnes	1966	Monument
Jigsaw Puzzle	Barry Sadler	Paul Parnes	1967	RCA Victor
Johnny Will #35 on Billboard Hot 100 chart; #4 on U.K. charts	Pat Boone	Fred Tobias	1961	Dot Records
Johnny Will (Geld Wie Heu)	Gerd Böttcher	Fred Tobias, Hans Bradtke	1962	Decca Germany
Johnny Will	Foster & Allen	Fred Tobias	1994	Telstar Ireland
Journey Of Love	Jeanne & Janie (Jeanne Black)	Matt Williams	1960	Capitol
Juanita Jones #13 on Billboard Country chart	Stu Phillips	Paul Parnes	1967	RCA Victor
Julie Doesn't Love Me Anymore	Sammy Salvo	Jimmy Krondes	1958	RCA Victor
Last Happy Song #22 on Billboard Adult Contemporary chart	Hillside Singers	Paul Parnes	1972	Metromedia
Last Happy Song	Peters & Lee	Paul Parnes	1973	Philips Records U.K.

Song	Artist	Co-writer	Year	Record Label
Let's Pretend #11 on U.K. charts; B-side of "To Sir With Love"	Lulu	Paul Parnes	1967	Columbia U.K.
Let's Pretend	Donna Loren	Paul Parnes	1967	Reprise
Let's Pretend	Marilyn Michaels	Paul Parnes	1967	ABC Records
Let's Pretend	Margaret Whiting	Paul Parnes	1967	London
Let's Pretend	The Sandpipers	Paul Parnes	1967	Star
Let's Pretend	Sharifah Aini	Paul Parnes	1981	EMI Malaysia
Let's Talk This Over (Before It's Too Late)	Carl Smith	Fred Tobias	1963	Columbia
Life Goes On	Bobby Vinton	Paul Parnes	1964	Epic
Live Young Theme song for the film *Palm Springs Weekend*	Troy Donahue	Larry Kusik	1966	Warner Bros.
Live Young	John Gary	Larry Kusik	1968	RCA Camden
Long As The Rose Is Red Female answer to "Roses Are Red" #62 on Billboard Hot 100 chart #15 on Billboard Adult Contemporary chart	Florraine Darlin	Al Byron	1962	Epic
Million And One Times, A	Bernd Spier	Jack Reardon	1965	Columbia
Miserable Me	Molly Bee	Paul Parnes	1965	MGM
My Wall Came Tumblin Down	Kitty Wells & Red Foley	No Co-writer	1967	Decca
New Breed, The	Jackie Wilson	Jack Reardon	1963	Brunswick/U.S. Coral/U.K.

Song	Artist	Co-writer	Year	Record Label
Next Step Is Love, The #32 on Billboard Hot 100 #5 on Billboard Adult Contemporary #57 on Billboard Country chart Featured in the film *Elvis, That's The Way It Is*	Elvis Presley	Paul Parnes	1970	RCA Victor
No Trespassing	Helen Shapiro	Fred Tobias	1963	Columbia U.K.
No Tresspassing (Hän On Verkossani)	Anki Lindqvist	Fred Tobias, Juha Vainio	1963	Columbia Finland
Note In Box #9, The #62 on Billboard Country chart	Stu Phillips	Paul Parnes	1968	RCA Victor
Nothing Moves Me Like You Do	Ruff Diamond	Paul Parnes	1967	Columbia
Only Way To Love, The	Frankie Lymon	Jimmy Krondes	1958	Roulette
Ooh Baby (Love Got Me Again)	Judy Somerville	Lea Jane Berinati	1989	DUBL Recordings
Open Up Your Garden Gate	Kenny Adams	Jack Reardon	1959	Seco Records
One Red Rose	Johnny Tillotson	Paul Parnes	1965	MGM
Ordinary Person, An	Anita Sheer	Paul Parnes	1966	Verve Folkways
Our Love	Tab Hunter	Gratien Ouellette	1956	Warner Bros.
Our World #70 on Billboard Country chart	Johnny Tillotson	Paul Parnes	1965	MGM
Our World (Si Tout Change)	Johnny Hallyday	Paul Parnes, Jacques Chaumelle	1963	Philips Records France
Our World (Vår Värld)	Anna-Lena	Paul Parnes, Anna-Lena Löfgren	1966	Metronome Sweden

Song	Artist	Co-writer	Year	Record Label
Our World (Onze Wereld)	Greetje Mona	Paul Parnes, Van Aleda, Ke Riema	1966	Palette Netherlands
Pardon Me	Annisteen Allen	No Co-writer	1957	Decca
Pass the Time of Day	Bonnie Guitar	Paul Parnes	1970	Decca
Picture On My Wall	Diana Cole	Al Byron	1959	Strand
Please Don't Take The Children From Me	Lorene Mann	Paul Parnes	1966	RCA Victor
Poppa's Home-Made Wine	Pat Cooper	Paul Parnes	1966	United Artists
Price I Had To Pay, The	Penny DeHaven	Paul Parnes	1969	United Artists
P.T.A., The	The Coasters	Fred Tobias	1963	Atco
Roses Are Red, My Love #1 on Billboard Hot 100 chart #15 on U.K. chart	Bobby Vinton	Al Byron	1962	Epic
Roses Are Red, My Love	Freddie Fender	Al Byron	1962	Capitol
Roses Are Red, My Love #3 on U.K. charts	Ronnie Carroll	Al Byron	1962	Philips Records U.K.
Roses Are Red, My Love	David Macbeth	Al Byron	1962	Piccadilly U.K.
Roses Are Red, My Love	Billy Vaughn	Al Byron	1962	Dot/U.S. London/U.K.
Roses Are Red, My Love	Johnny Brunette & the Johnny Mann Singers	Al Byron	1962	Liberty Records
Roses Are Red, My Love	Bobby Rydell & the Bernie Lowe Orchestra	Al Byron	1962	Cameo
Roses Are Red, My Love	Al Caiola & the Manhattan Strings	Al Byron	1962	United Artists

Song	Artist	Co-writer	Year	Record Label
Roses Are Red, My Love	Shelley Fabares	Al Byron	1962	Colpix Records
Roses Are Red, My Love	Dickey Lee	Al Byron	1962	Smash Records
Roses Are Red (Rosen Sind Rot)	Caterina Valente	Al Byron, Hans Bradtke	1962	Decca German
Roses Are Red, My Love (Le Rose Sono Rossa)	Johnny Dorelli	Al Byron, Panzeri	1962	Bravo Italian
Roses Are Red, My Love	Jim Reeves	Al Byron	1963	RCA Victor
Roses Are Red, My Love	The Wilburn Brothers	Al Byron	1963	Decca
Roses Are Red, My Love	Brian Poole & the Tremeloes	Al Byron	1963	Ace of Clubs U.K.
Roses Are Red, My Love	Ferlin Husky	Al Byron	1963	Capitol
Roses Are Red, My Love	Bobby Goldsboro	Al Byron	1964	United Artists
Roses Are Red, My Love (Rosas Rojas)	Los Hermanos Carrion	Al Byron, H. González	1964	CBS Spanish
Roses Are Red, My Love	Pete Drake (Steel Guitarist)	Al Byron	1965	Smash Records
Roses Are Red, My Love	Pat Boone	Al Byron	1965	Dot Records
Roses Are Red, My Love (Crvene Ruže)	Ivica Šerfezi & Ansambl Crveni Koralji	Al Byron,	1967	Jugoton Croatia
Roses Are Red, My Love	Patty Duke	Al Byron	1967	United Artists
Roses Are Red, My Love	Slim Whitman	Al Byron	1967	Capitol
Roses Are Red, My Love 玫瑰花香	Zhuang Xue Fang	Al Byron,	1967	Ruby Records Chinese

Song	Artist	Co-writer	Year	Record Label
Roses Are Red, My Love	Sonny James	Al Byron	1968	Capitol
Roses Are Red, My Love	Liz Anderson	Al Byron	1969	RCA
Roses Are Red, My Love	Bobby Bare	Al Byron	1972	Bear Family
Roses Are Red, My Love	Leroy Van Dyke	Al Byron	1978	Plantation
Roses Are Red, My Love	Daniel O'Donnell	Al Byron	2003	Ritz Records Ireland
Round In Circles	Johnny Tillotson	Paul Parnes	1967	MGM
Saturday Night With My Girl	Dorian Burton	No Co-writer	1958	Decca
School Bells A New York "Doo-wop" hit	Nicky and the Nobles	Jimmy Krondes	1958	Gone
She Came On Like Lightnin'	Reba McEntire	Jerry Holland	1994	Mercury
Sidewalk Sweethearts	The Coquettes with Ray Charles & his Orchestra	Paul Parnes	1957	Columbia
She's Stayin' Inside With Me	Fabian	Fred Tobias	1962	Dot Records
Something Blue	Elvis Presley	Al Byron	1962	RCA Victor
Something Blue (C'est À Nous)	Eddy Mitchell	A. Byron, E. Mitchell, R. Berent	1962	Barclay France
Speak, Sugar, Speak	The Lennon Sisters	Fred Tobias	1963	Dot Records
Start The World Spinning	Sherri Weine	Fred Tobias	1965	World Artists
Start The World Spinning	The Diamond Twins	Fred Tobias	1966	His Master's Voice
Strange Feeling	Jerry Mason	Jimmy Krondes	1959	Kapp Records
Suffer Now Baby, Suffer	Flip Black	Paul Parnes	1966	Jubilee Records

Song	Artist	Co-writer	Year	Record Label
Summer Souvenirs #68 on Billboard Hot 100 chart	Karl Hammel, Jr.	Jimmy Krondes	1961	Arliss Records
Sweet, Sweet Reason	Ed Ames	Paul Parnes	1970	RCA
Sweet, Sweet Reason	Solomon Burke	Paul Parnes	1972	MGM
Take A Look	Short Twins	Woody Harris, Jack Reardon	1958	Eagle Records
Ten Most Wanted Men	Spencer Trask	Al Byron	1962	Keys Records
That Room In The Corner Of The House	Bobby Lord	No Co-Writer	1965	Hickory
That's When It Hurts The Most	Johnny Tillotson	Larry Kusik	1964	MGM Records
There Is No Joy Left In Milwaukee	Frankie Yankovic & the Yanks	Paul Parnes	1966	Columbia
They Could Be Wrong	Buddy Brooks AKA Barry Mann	J. Reardon, D. Fleischhacker	1958	Eagle Records
There's A Fool Born Every Minute #16 on Billboard Country chart	Skeeter Davis	Paul Parnes	1968	RCA Victor
There's A Warm Welcome Waiting For You	Glenn Douglas Tubb	Fred Tobias	1964	Limelight
Think Summer #17 on Billboard Adult Contemporary chart	Ed Ames & Marilyn Maye	Paul Parnes	1970	RCA
Think Summer #20 on Billboard Adult Contemporary chart #21 on Billboard Country chart	Roy Clark	Paul Parnes	1976	DOT Records
Tiny Spaceman	Wes Bryan	Jack Reardon	1957	United Artists

Song	Artist	Co-writer	Year	Record Label
Tiny Spaceman	Bill Carlisle	Jack Reardon	1957	RCA Victor
This Is Your Day	Burl Ives	Fred Tobias	1964	Decca
Thunderbolt	Sammy Turner & the Twisters	Paul Parnes	1959	Big Top
Too Good To Be True	Jim Ed Brown	Paul Parnes	1967	RCA Victor
Two Minus One	Micki Fuhrman	Al Byron	1981	MCA Records
Usually You	Bobby Diamond	Paul Parnes	1966	Columbia
Valerie A big New York "Doo-wop" hit	Mello Kings	Jimmy Krondes	1958	Herald
What's A Nice Guy Doing In A Place Like This	The Strommen Brothers	Marty Kupersmith	1983	Monument
When #5 on Billboard Hot 100 chart; #1 on U.K charts for 5 weeks	The Kalin Twins	Jack Reardon	1958	Decca
When (Wenn)	James Brothers	Reardon, Blecher, & May	1958	Polydor Germany
When	Pierre Cavalli	Jack Reardon	1959	Jamie
When	The Kaye Sisters	Jack Reardon	1959	Philips Records U.K.
When	The Fraternity Brothers	Jack Reardon	1959	Verve Records
When (Organ Version)	Lenny Dee	Jack Reardon	1959	Decca
When (Ven)	Milan Chladil a Yvetta Simonová	Jack Reardon, Václav Jelínek	1959	Supraphon Czechoslovakia
When #3 on U.K., charts	Showaddywaddy	Jack Reardon	1977	Arista U.K.
When	Anita Sarawak	Jack Reardon	1977	EMI Singapore
When	Lisa del Bo	Jack Reardon	2000	Piet Roelen Belgium

Song	Artist	Co-writer	Year	Record Label
When	Daniel O'Donnell	Jack Reardon	2004	DMG TV U.K. & Europe
When I Dance With You	Millie Small	Paul Parnes, Andre Livernaux	1968	Fontana U.K.
When I'm Near My Girl	Brian Davies	Jimmy Krondes	1959	Dot Records
When Love Is Gone Theme song in the French film Bilitis	Samantha Sang	Bryan Wells, Francis Lai	1977	Private Stock Records
When You Hurt Me	Paul Peek	Fred Tobias	1963	Mercury
Worried Guy #37 on Billboard Hot 100 chart	Johnny Tillotson	Jack Reardon	1964	MGM Records
You Know What	Chad & Jeremy	Paul Parnes	1965 1966	World Artists/ U.S. Ember/U.K.

BIBLIOGRAPHY

Bronson, Fred, *The Billboard Book of Number 1 Hits,* Billboard Books, 2003.

Broven, John, *Record Makers and Breakers: Voices of the Independent Rock 'n' Roll Pioneers,* University of Illinois Press, 2009.

Clark, Dick, *Rock, Roll & Remember,* Thomas Y. Crowell Company, 1976.

Dannen, Frederic, *Hit Men: Power Brokers and Fast Money Inside the Music Business,* Times Books, Random House, 1990.

Leigh, Spencer, *Buddy Holly: Learning the Game,* McNidder & Grace, 2019.

Palm, Carl Magnus. *ABBA Blog #10: For Old Time's Sake, Man!* Mar 30, 2012. www.carlmagnuspalm.com [accessed February 2020]

Wilkinson, Tony. "I Was Part of the 50s—The Paul Evans Story." *American Music Magazine*, 92, June 2002, p. 4.

Zirpolo, Michael P. *Manhattan's Brill Building, A Jazz Showcase and Musical Shrine.* Swing & Beyond, January 27, 2017. https://swingandbeyond.com/2017/01/27/swingin-at-the-brill-building/ [accessed February 2020]

INDEX

ACKNOWLEDGMENTS

"Songwriter" is one word, and "book writer" is two words. That's because there's very little similarity between the two. So I had a lot of help tackling this, my very first book.

I want to thank the following people for their most necessary help:

Andy and Caroline Peden Smith for their belief that I could come up to McNidder & Grace's high standards, and for their encouragement when it was most needed. Thanks, too, to Spencer Leigh for introducing me to them.

Paul Sklar for his always dependable legal counseling.

John Broven, Gary Theroux, Johnny Vallis and Sam Szczepanski for helping to keep my facts straight.

My niece, Lonnie Friedman, for reading a rough draft of my first chapter, and making style suggestions that I accepted and continued to follow.

Ron Lockhart and George Russo for helping me recall how things worked in the early days of the computer and the Internet.

Stanley Mills for letting me pick through his remarkable memory.

Allan Sniffen for his knowledge of the top DJs of my youth.

Warren Schatz for his stories of Associated Studio engineers.

Roger Easterby for sharing his knowledge of the UK charts and labels.

Lea Jane Berinati Burie for sharing her knowledge of Nashville's music scene.

Mark Fried for suggesting *Happy Go Lucky Me* for the book's title

Marilyn Holot Kane for being my fan club president, so many years ago.

Paul Rolnick for helping me to stick around as a music creator a bit longer than I thought possible.

And, of course, I am grateful to my friends, co-writers, and business associates who helped me get from here to there, easing my journey through the music business.

I've saved the biggest thank you for last. To my beautiful and talented wife and partner, Susan. I know that the phrase "beautiful and talented" is overused in acknowledgments, but what can I do? She is what she is.

There is no way that I could have come close to writing this book without her by my side each and every step of the undertaking. Susan helped me edit *Happy Go Lucky Me* and put many, many hours into doing research for it. She put together the list of artists who recorded my songs. Over the years she safely held onto photos and memorabilia that you can see scattered throughout *Happy Go Lucky Me,* and those keepsakes brought lots of memories back to life for me.

I met Susan on a blind date in 1972 and we've travelled the world together and loved each other ever since.